"So why are you here today, Kate?"

"I had to make an honest woman of myself and return your sweatshirt."

Casey laughed lightly. "A two-hundred-mile roundtrip to return a stained, used sweatshirt? Seems like a lot of work." She looked over the remaining trees in the field. "That should do it. The others are big enough to survive the winter." She laid the shovel down and took off her gloves. She reached a hand up and ran her fingers through her hair, then rolled her head from side to side and arched her shoulders. "Ready to load these bad boys up and get them back to the greenhouse?" Casey bent as if to hoist one of the containers of trees, but Kate caught her by the upper arm before she could pick it up.

Wordlessly, she turned Casey a quarter turn so that they were standing face to face, then drew her to her body. Ever so gently, she laid her lips on Casey's, not sure if the kiss would be returned or rejected. Casey pulled back and studied Kate's face. Whatever she saw there was enough; whatever sign she needed was provided. She pressed in tight against Kate and kissed her with a passion that she had been sure would never be granted to her again.

And when Kate returned that passion in kind, they both knew that the clocks inside their broken hearts could finally start marking the passing of time.

Visit

Bella Books

at

BellaBooks.com

or call our toll-free number

1-800-729-4992

Picture Perfect

Jane Vollbrecht

Bella
BOOKS

2005

Bella Books, Inc.
P.O. Box 10543
Tallahassee, FL 32302

Printed in the United States of America on acid-free paper
First Edition

Editor: Pamela Berard
Cover designer: Sandy Knowles

ISBN 1-59493-015-5

For my big sisters, Mary and Kathryn. They read to me and showed me the power and the magic of words.

Acknowledgments

Special thanks to Pamela Berard, my editor. She was brave enough to take on a rookie's manuscript. Her assistance was invaluable.

Abundant gratitude to Becky Arbogast at Bella Books for her patience and her suggestions. Her help made this book possible.

Heartfelt (and heartbroken) thanks to Ralph and Ben and Chet and all of the other fathers who, in their struggles with dementia, lit paths we never imagined we would have to tread.

I credit my brothers, Paul and Tony, for providing me, without intending to do so, much needed diversions and distractions while I was working on the book, and I also thank them for their help with historical and current land prices.

Sincere thanks to friends and family members who cheered— most in support, some in surprise—when they heard I was writing a book.

And finally, endless thanks to Kathleen, my infinitely better half, who always encourages me to pursue my dreams.

Chapter 1

"Do you mind if I turn the air conditioner off and open the sliding glass door? That way, we can listen to the rain."

Nora didn't wait for an answer. She flipped the lever on the thermostat and slid both patio doors open wide. The afternoon shower cascaded off the trees and deck railing, sounding again as it splashed down on the ground below. The steady tattoo of the raindrops on the roof set up a pulsing counterbeat to contrast the syncopated rhythm off the leaves and redwood.

"Do you want some tea?" Burr, Nora's husband, asked as he passed through the living room on his way to the covered deck.

"No thanks, dear," Nora replied. "How about you, Kate?"

"No, I'm still full from lunch. Thanks anyway."

Nora and Kate watched out the screen door as Burr settled himself in one of the Brumby rockers beneath the cantilevered overhang. He had no more than gotten seated when he was on his feet and headed back in.

"Can I get either of you something to drink?" he offered as he closed the screen behind him.

"No, we're fine, sweetie. Thanks."

Burr ambled off to the back part of the house and then re-emerged in less than a minute.

"I'm going to get a beer. Would you like something, Nora? How about you, uh . . ."

"Kate," Nora supplied. "No, Burr, we don't need anything. Are you going to go sit on the deck and read?"

"Yes."

Emptyhanded, Burr went back to the deck and resumed the chair he had vacated moments before.

"He'll pick up a book in a minute and then he'll doze off." Nora sounded apologetic.

"Can he hear us, Nora?"

"No, he's had a hearing problem for years, but he has adamantly refused to get a hearing aid. With the rain falling like that, I'm sure he can't hear a word we say."

"I guess you tried to warn me about this, didn't you?"

"How's that, Kate?"

"When I called a couple of weeks ago to ask about coming up to see you, you made lots of references to 'Burr relies on me for most everything these days,' and other sideways remarks about 'we're really starting to show our age,' and things like that."

"Well, I hadn't seen you in years, Kate. I didn't want you to be totally surprised by what you'd find here."

"So how long has Burr been having memory problems?"

"Oh, I don't suppose I really know. It's not like one day he was fine and the next day he was like this. It's been coming on gradually for at least a couple of years. I guess it's been at least six months that I've known for sure that this isn't just simple forgetfulness."

"Have you seen a doctor?"

"I doubt that there's a doctor between here and Asheville who's got the first clue about dealing with Alzheimer's or whatever it is that's eating Burr's brain."

"Couldn't you take him to Emory or someplace down in Atlanta?"

"He fights tooth and claw about going to see any doctor anytime. As best I can tell, he's perfectly fine physically, so I can't use that as a wedge to get him there. Some days, I think he realizes that his mind just isn't working right, and that scares the fool out of him, so he's all the more reluctant to go see a doctor and have it confirmed."

"What about you, Nora? How are you holding up?"

Kate and Nora had met when Kate joined the accounting firm where Nora had been working for a number of years. Despite their noticeable age difference, the two women had forged a long-standing bond. Nora had helped Kate get her footing, both professionally and personally, and because of that, Kate had an abiding affection for Nora. Likewise, Nora was very fond of Kate and regarded her almost as another daughter.

Nora gazed out the window for a long time before answering. "Well, the kids have been a big help."

"That's good. Where are they by now? I've long since lost track."

"Burleson, Junior—BJ—is still in California trying to prove that 'starving artist' isn't just a marketing ploy; Darren and his second wife are south of Atlanta. He's currently between jobs, but he's got good computer skills, so we're hoping he'll land another job soon. As for the girls, Christine and her husband and daughter are in north Florida. She's doing very well selling real estate. Margie, my baby, is in Atlanta with her husband and son—that's his kindergarten graduation picture over there." Nora pointed to the top of the TV at a photograph of a smiling, blond child. "And Casey is here in Delano, working for a landscaping company."

"Really? How did Casey end up here? I thought she was a big city girl."

"She was, but a few years ago, uh . . ."—Nora seemed to struggle to find the right words—"there were some big changes in her life and she came up here to—what's that phrase kids used to use? Oh yes, to find herself. One thing led to another, and now she's got a place of her own, a dog, two cats, and a car note."

"The kids all know about Burr's condition?"

"It would be hard to miss, Kate. How long did it take you? Five minutes?"

"I didn't know how often they got home to see you."

"Well, the girls and Darren are here every couple of months. BJ makes it about once a year—if his father and I buy his plane ticket. And of course, we see Casey at least once or twice every week now that she lives just down the road."

A low rumble of thunder growled in the distance. Nora and Kate glanced toward the deck. Burr's chin was resting on his chest, his book still clenched upside down in his hands resting in his lap.

"It's pretty up here, Nora." Kate gazed out over the treetops, black from the moisture, toward the ridge of mountains just discernable to the north and west.

"Pretty lonely, pretty remote, pretty much not what I had in mind for retirement." She couldn't keep the edge of rancor out of her voice.

"I thought the plan all along was to get out of Atlanta when Burr retired from the aeronautics firm."

"It was, but we were supposed to move to Lake Lanier, not clear up here in no-man's-land."

"What happened to Lanier?"

"I'm hardly the one to ask. We had an option on a piece of lakefront property, but something went wrong. Burr never told me exactly what happened. One day, he just up and announced that, after retirement, we were moving to Delano, North Carolina."

"He didn't talk it over with you first?"

"Oh right." Nora snorted. "Just like he consulted me on every other decision that affected me and the rest of the family."

"I guess I remember that he wasn't exactly big on partnership and democracy."

"No, more like 'my way or the highway.'"

"So, here you are in the mountains of North Carolina, living in a town you don't like where you have very few friends, and your hus-

4

band is suffering from some form of dementia, with no appropriate accessible medical care in the vicinity."

"That about sums it up," Nora concurred.

"So what are you going to do, Nora?"

Again, there was a long pause before Nora replied. "What I've always done, I suppose. Put on my happy face and make the best of things."

Another clap of thunder, this one very nearby, shook the windows. It seemed to be the cloudburst's parting gesture. The rain quickly subsided from downpour to drizzle to mist. Burr was roused from his slumber by the peal. He opened the screen and stepped inside.

"Who'd like some tea?"

Despite the brightening sky, Kate sensed a gathering storm.

Chapter 2

"You remember Kate Bingham, don't you, Casey?" Nora threaded her way amongst the pots of monkey grass and flowering annuals.

Nora, Burr, and Kate had tried to make conversation back at the house, but Burr's endless repeating of himself prompted Nora to suggest that she and Kate take a drive over to the nursery where Casey was working. Kate drove while Nora called out the turns. After a twenty-minute drive over several unmarked gravel roads, they came to a sign for Frank's Landscape and Nursery. They made their way down a long hill to an open area tucked in one of the many valleys in the mountains of western North Carolina. The business consisted of one large tan metal building and half a dozen other smaller outbuildings scattered around a rutted parking lot. The open areas between and among the various buildings were lined with plants and flowers of every sort and color.

Casey Marsden looked up from the oakleaf hydrangea she was pruning as her mother approached. She shucked her work glove and dusted her palm against the fringe of her cut-off jeans.

"Sure, I remember Kate, but it's been ten or twelve years at least since we've seen each other." She offered her hand to Kate. "How've you been? Good to see you."

Kate clasped Casey's outstretched hand. "Fine, thanks. It's good to see you, too."

"I'd apologize for how grungy I look, but the truth is, this is about as clean as I ever am anymore." Casey grinned widely as she released Kate's hand. "Sometimes I wish the old biddy I worked for when I was a salesclerk at the department store at Northlake Mall could see what I look like day in and day out. She used to have a cow if there was so much as a chip in my nail polish. Now I'm lucky if I don't have cow manure under every nail." Casey tossed her head back and laughed out loud.

"I take it you find landscaping to be a better occupation for you, Casey?"

"You bet. I'm outside almost all day every day. At the end of the day, I'm tired, but in a good way. When I worked at the mall all I had to show for it was sore feet and an aching back from wearing those stupid sissy girl shoes all day."

Casey shifted her gaze from Kate to Nora. "How's Daddy doing?"

"Oh, you know. About like every other day." Nora's eyes lingered on her child. She shook her head slightly as if to move past a thought she'd rather not dwell on. "He said he'd be coming by here later to pick up some mulch so that we can do those rose beds we were working on last weekend."

"Mother, we've talked about this dozens of times. Do you really think it's safe for him to drive, especially alone?" Nora shot her daughter a look that Kate caught and interpreted to mean, "Don't talk about this in public."

"I mean, wouldn't it be better if I just brought the mulch over the next time I come by the house?" Casey continued. "He can hardly lift those heavy bags anymore."

"Well, you know your father needs to keep busy, honey. Some of those nice young men who work in the storage building will help him load up when he gets here. You just keep an eye out for him, OK? And maybe you could give me a call when he leaves so that I'll know that he's on his way home."

Casey looked as though she were about to say something more to her mother, but then thought better of it.

"Do you do much gardening, Kate?" she asked as she pulled her gloves back on. "I can get you some great deals on our overstocks."

"No, despite having grown up on a farm, about the only thing I raise these days is an occasional glass of wine. My fourteenth-floor condominium doesn't exactly have a good spot for a flower garden."

"So you're still in Atlanta?" Casey resumed her pruning; Nora wandered off and inspected the pots of canna lilies several rows over from where the three women had been standing.

"Actually, I just got back. I think the last time I saw you was when your parents were still living down there and you were working as a bartender somewhere in the Underground. Since then, I've moved two or three times. Now I'm back in Atlanta and hope to make it my home for a while."

"Are you still working for Dewey, Screwum, and Howe?" Casey snickered.

"Yes, I'm still with the accounting firm where I first met your mother—Lord, it must be twenty years ago—but the phone book lists us a little less sarcastically."

"I know I shouldn't be so mean. They gave Mother a good retirement package when she left. I know she still misses a lot of her friends down in Atlanta."

"She was telling me a little bit about life up here in Delano earlier. Seems like retirement didn't pan out quite as she had envisioned." Kate shifted another potted oakleaf hydrangea nearer to Casey. "Here, this one needs a shave and a little off the top, too."

"Thanks." Casey pivoted the plant she had been pruning out of the way and started on the new one. "No, Mom's pretty miserable these days. We've all been kind of worried about her ever since they moved up here. And now this stuff with my dad . . ." Casey left the sentence unfinished.

"Your mother didn't seem too eager to talk much about it with me. I guess I can't blame her. It's been years since we'd seen each other."

"Wouldn't have mattered if you'd seen her every day for five years. Other than an occasional superficial conversation, she won't even talk to me or my brothers and sisters about it. It's almost like she thinks that not talking about it will somehow make it not be what's happening." Casey glanced up and saw Nora approaching. "Better drop it for now," she said softly.

"I think I saw your father's van pulling in down the hill, Casey. Maybe you can go meet him and show him how to get to the loading dock by the storage building." As Casey strode off to try to intercept her father, Nora turned her attention to Kate. "Since you drove us over here in your car, Kate, if you wouldn't mind, I think I'll just ride home with Burr and you can go on back to Atlanta from here. Casey can tell you how to get back to the main road."

Nora hastened off to join her husband and daughter, leaving Kate amid the hydrangeas. Kate looked across the nursery lot to where the Marsden family had gathered. She could catch an occasional snippet of conversation.

"No, Burr, you have to turn the handle before you can open the door."

"No, Daddy, not the plants, the bags."

"No, sir, I didn't know your daughter's name was Christine. I thought it was Casey."

Burr looked overwhelmed and confused. Nora looked embarrassed and distant. Casey looked young and muscular and very much the one in control of the situation.

Kate lingered a moment and allowed herself to study Casey more carefully. She had first met Casey shortly after she and Nora had become coworkers. She remembered being struck all those years ago by how attractive Casey was. The intervening years had only added to her charms. Then, as now, Casey didn't use makeup but rather had a natural beauty that radiated around her. Her light blonde hair framed her face and set off her strong jaw line. Although Kate couldn't see Casey's eyes from where she was standing, she had seen them just a few minutes earlier and had been reminded of how their depth and warmth had caught her attention the first time they met. Casey's eyes were blue, like Nora's, but they had a hint of green and gold, too, which definitely made them Casey's most intriguing feature.

Kate roused herself from her reflections and pulled her keys from the pocket of her khakis. She set off toward her car on the other side of the nursery lot. She was confident she could find her way back to the highway to make the two-hour drive back to Atlanta.

Sadly, what she had seen that day left her confident of something else, too. The Marsden family would never find its way back to how it had been.

Chapter 3

"DeWitt, Scroggins, and Howell. Kate Bingham speaking. May I help you?"

"Don't you mean 'Dewey, Screwum, and Howe?' Hi, Kate. It's Casey Marsden."

"Casey? What a surprise."

"Am I catching you at a bad time?"

"No, not at all. I just finished with a client and was about to go to lunch."

"Good. I was hoping I could talk to you about something."

"Of course, Casey." Kate paused. "Is everything all right with your parents?"

"Yes. Well, no. Umm, I mean I guess that's what I wanted to talk to you about."

Kate waited silently.

"I'm really worried about them both, Kate. You saw what it was like when you were up here a couple of weeks ago."

"I wasn't sure just how bad things are. I know your dad seems to be having a lot of trouble remembering things," Kate ventured.

"Yeah, like his name and where he lives and that he's supposed to wear pants."

"Has he suddenly gotten worse?"

"Actually, no, I don't think so. It's just that I'm tired of playing Mother's game that this is just a little problem that will evaporate if we mutter the right incantations." Casey gave a half-hearted laugh. "It's almost like Daddy gets a little bit worse and Mother gets a lot worse."

"Sorry, I'm not sure I follow what you mean."

Kate heard Casey draw in a deep breath.

"I know it's a lot to ask, but I wondered if you'd consider coming back up to Delano—maybe this weekend. If you spend a little more time with the two of them, I think you'll get a better idea of what's going on." Casey hesitated a moment. "And all of this would be lots easier to talk about face to face."

"Gee, Casey, I'm not sure what it is that you think I can do. I'm an accountant, not a doctor."

"I know. But Mother really thinks highly of you. I guess I'm just hoping that maybe she'd listen to you. No one in the family seems to be able to crack the shell."

"Well . . ."

"Think it over for a day or two if you want. I can call you back tomorrow or the next day to see what you've decided."

"I don't mean to seem unconcerned, Casey. I'm happy to do what I can. I just don't know what that might be."

"Truth be told, Kate, I don't really know what you could do either." Casey sighed audibly. "I suppose I'm just feeling sorry for myself."

"Oh? How's that?"

"I see my parents a couple of times a week; I watch them struggling to pretend that everything is just peachy. Then, if Mother gets feeling overwhelmed, when Daddy's out of earshot, she calls me, but almost every time, it's like she chickens out and doesn't really tell me everything I need to know. That makes me feel like I need to try to do something—anything—to help the situation, but I don't know what to do, so I call my brothers or sisters, but I don't have anything specific to pass on to them. That makes them think I'm some kind of over-reactive worrywart crying wolf all the time. And round and round it goes."

"And somehow you think that I can put the brakes on the carousel?"

"Hey, my mother always said you were the brightest apprentice to come into that accounting office. She predicted that you'd set the place on its ear, and you did." Casey laughed lightly. "What the hell, I figured it was worth a shot." She took a breath and went on. "Besides, I only got to spend a few minutes with you when you were up here a couple of weeks ago. Maybe if you came up again, we could spend some time with my parents, and then I could treat you to dinner to say thanks. What do you say, Kate?"

"Have the leaves started to turn up there?"

"Now that you mention it, yes, they have. All of the dogwoods and sourwoods are already bright red and the maples and poplars aren't far behind."

"All right, Casey, I'll plan to drive up to Delano on Saturday. I've got to tell you, I don't think that there's a single thing in all of God's great earth that I can do to make much difference for your mom and dad, but your mother has been a loyal friend for two decades or more. Even if all I can do is listen to you recount the woes and horrors while looking at the autumn leaves, so be it."

"That's great, Kate. I'll be looking forward to seeing you. What time do you think you'll get here?"

"I'll blow out of Atlanta around eight Saturday morning. That should put me up there shortly after ten."

"Come by Frank's and we'll go to Mother's from there. Do you think you can find the nursery where I work again?"

"Sure. I'll carry my cell phone just in case I get lost."

"I think it would be better if we don't tell my parents that you're coming. That way, you'll see them without Mother having a chance to hang all her window dressings." Casey cleared her throat, then continued. "Does that sound like I'm being mean, Kate?"

"No, more like you think there are two problems, not just one."

"It will be good to have someone help me look at all of this objectively—if that's possible."

"Well, I'll do my best, Casey."

"Hey, thanks, Kate. It took me three weeks to work up the courage to call you. I'm really glad you're coming."

"Sure thing. See you Saturday."

Kate replaced the phone in its cradle and then pulled open the large lower drawer in the credenza behind her desk. She took her wallet from her attaché and tucked a twenty and a credit card into the inside breast pocket of her gray pinstriped suit. She scanned her appointment book before pushing back from her desk. As she passed through the outer office, she paused at her secretary's desk.

"Bernice, cancel my Saturday breakfast meeting with Mr. Howell. Tell him that I need to take care of a family matter and that I'll be out of town for the weekend. See what you can work out with his secretary for rescheduling sometime next week."

Kate caught the elevator to the lobby and wandered out into the warm afternoon, its early autumn sun washing over downtown Atlanta.

Chapter 4

"If this is your idea of a little bit of color, I wonder what your idea of full-fledged autumn foliage would be like."

"When I talked to you earlier in the week, Kate, I swear the leaves had just started to turn. Then we had two nights of hard frost, and suddenly everything is at peak. Did you have lots of leaf-lookers on the road with you on the drive up?"

"No, it wasn't too bad. I got out of town before all the Buckhead soccer moms figured out that this was the weekend to load up the van and head north." Kate wrapped her arms around herself and hunched her shoulders toward her ears. She and Casey were standing outside one of the open ends of the main building at Frank's Landscape and Nursery. Although it was midmorning, the sun was just making its way above the trees that stood on the eastern ridge surrounding the nursery. The cloudless sky shimmered with the angled sunlight. Kate's bright pink cotton turtleneck and sleeveless knit vest had seemed sufficient when she left Atlanta but were proving inadequate in the mountain air. "I hadn't thought it was this chilly."

"Probably wasn't down in the city. You've climbed more than a thousand feet to get up here. It's often ten to twenty degrees cooler here than it is in Atlanta. I've got an extra sweatshirt in my truck. I'll get it for you." Casey sprinted off to the far end of the parking lot where her well-used Nissan pickup sat. Kate was suddenly aware of her reaction to Casey's appearance. She recalled how she had stood and studied Casey from across the parking lot on the day that she watched the Marsden family congregate at the storage building when Burr came to pick up the bags of mulch. Up close, she could see that her assessment of Casey's strong, trim body was right on the mark. The physical labor of lifting, shoveling, hauling, and planting had produced a toned, almost sculpted, body readily apparent from the perfect fit of her faded jeans and chamois cloth shirt. Casey obviously had spent the summer outdoors. Her face was still tanned; her blonde hair showed evidence of having been bleached a shade lighter by the sun.

"Nora has raised quite a beauty; she's pretty as a picture," Kate thought as Casey returned.

"Here, put this on. It's clean; just ignore those stains. You know that once the red clay up here claims an article of clothing, it's tainted for life." Casey handed Kate an oversized navy blue sweatshirt. Kate slipped it over her head and ran her fingers through her light brown shoulder-length hair to free it from the crew neck.

Casey did a quick physical inventory of the woman who would be spending the day with her. She loved the color of Kate's hair. She decided the English language needed a new word that described the color, which was somewhere between brown and blonde. Maybe they could name it Bingham blonde-brown or something. Kate's brown eyes were the sort that a careless person could get lost in. They were soft and inviting, with just enough twinkle in them to suggest that Kate had a secret that she'd share, but only if the right person earned the privilege. Although Kate matched Casey's five-foot-seven-inch height, she was a slighter build, not really delicate, Casey concluded, but more what she would describe as sort of petite butch.

"Thanks. I should have brought a jacket. Nothing but a dumb flatlander, I guess." Kate chuckled as she turned and met Casey's gaze.

"Give it an hour or two, and it will warm up nicely. It only stays cool till about noon." Casey looked away briefly, then caught Kate's eye again. "So, are you ready for another day of my dad's version of twenty questions? Once you get the hang of it, it's easy. Just remember that he always asks the same question twenty times."

It was Kate's turn to look away. "I don't know if you know this, Casey, but my dad had a condition that was something like your dad's." She wanted to say more but the sudden lump in her throat kept her silent.

"No, I'm sure I didn't know that. Did my mother know?"

Kate swallowed hard and pushed the words past what was left of the knot in her windpipe. "I doubt it. It was fifteen years ago that your mother and I worked together. She and I always exchanged Christmas cards and sort of kept in touch that way, but this wasn't the sort of thing I could put in a Christmas card. My dad didn't get sick until several years after I had left the Atlanta office." She scanned the horizon like she was looking for the next line in her script. "I was living in New Haven when he died. He's been gone a little more than six years now."

"I'm sorry, Kate. I had no idea." Casey reached over and laid her hand on Kate's forearm.

"It's OK. It taught me that death isn't always a bad thing." Kate's voice quivered as she spoke. She tossed her shoulders; Casey pulled her hand back from Kate's forearm. "Well, standing here probably isn't doing much good."

"No, I guess not." Casey studied Kate's face for a clue. "Are you sure you're willing to go through with this, Kate? I mean, if I had known about your dad . . ."

17

"It's fine. Really. Your mother was so good to me when I started at DS and H; I've always wanted a chance to try to repay her. I never pictured it being in a situation like this, though. It was really tough to see her so unhappy when I visited her last month."

"Just let me run inside and tell Gerry that I'm off the clock today. Frank already knows, but he doesn't always remember to tell his wife that he's given me the day off. I'll be right back." Casey hurried into the building. Kate watched as she had a brief conversation with the woman behind the checkout counter and then returned to join her.

"Better let me drive. Daddy gets upset when strange cars come into the yard. So far, he still recognizes my truck." Casey led the way to the dented red Nissan. "Maybe if we can get away from Mother and Daddy's before the day is shot, we can go for a ride through the hills in that soup can of yours." Casey canted her head toward Kate's deep green Volvo sedan as they passed it in the lot. "You don't mind leaving it here, do you?"

"No. I figure it's safer here than it is in the garage under my condo building. For sure it's better off here than in the open-air lot in Midtown. Just let me grab my cell phone and sunglasses."

Once they reached the truck, Casey opened the passenger door and held it for Kate as she climbed in. "I wiped all the dog hair off the seat before I left home this morning. It should be pretty clean." Casey walked around to the driver's side and slid onto the vinyl seat. She cocked her head so that she was facing Kate.

"Last chance to back out, Ms. Bingham. Want to cut your losses and run?"

"Nope. Like I told you on the phone on Tuesday, I don't know what I can do to be of any help, but I'm willing to give it a try."

"Well, then best of luck to both of us." Casey cranked the engine and they were on their way.

Chapter 5

"Don't try to spare my feelings, Kate. Give me your honest assessment."

The tree-covered mountainsides were ablaze with the reflected light from what was left of the sun's rays. Kate and Casey had spent nearly six hours with Burr and Nora. They left the Marsdens' house around four-thirty and had been driving for ten minutes, neither saying a word.

Kate stared out the side window of the pickup and pulled in a deep breath. She blew out a puff of air and began. "With everything that went on at your parents' house today, I know it sounds like a silly thing to mention, but I never dreamed I'd see your mother looking like that. When she was an account assistant at DS and H, she always looked like she had stepped right off the cover of some glamour magazine. If I hadn't known better, when I first saw her this morning, I'd have sworn she was a bag lady."

"What else?"

"Well, your mom always was one who liked to have a glass of wine with dinner or to tip back a couple of eggnogs at the office holiday party, but I hadn't pictured her as someone who'd be half-potted before lunch. Was it just my imagination, or had she been drinking before we got there?"

"If today was like most days, yeah, I'm sure she had."

"Has this been going on long, Casey?"

"Oh, I'm not sure." Casey sighed. "Once I started seeing Mother and Daddy regularly after I moved up here to Delano, it seemed to me that she was already drinking more than I had remembered. I'd say that it's only been about eight or ten months or so that it's been really out of control."

"I swear I wasn't snooping, but when I went to use the bathroom after lunch, I had such a headache that I opened the medicine cabinet looking for some aspirin. I thought I had made a wrong turn into a pharmacy. Your mother must have had six different prescriptions for tranquilizers in there."

"And if you'd looked in her nightstand, you'd have found the bottles of uppers that she has to take to get through the days when she's had too many of the tranquilizers."

"Like I told you on the phone the other day, I'm no doctor, but even I know that a steady diet of booze and pills isn't a very smart course of action, Casey."

"Not exactly a news flash, Bingham." Casey downshifted as they turned off the blacktop onto a narrow gravel road. "Now I guess you know why I wanted you to come up again."

"Well, since you've brought that up, actually, no, I don't. Wouldn't your brothers and sisters be the ones to bring in on this?"

"I've tried, Kate. But even though I always ask them not to tell Mother that they're coming, they always call ahead and ask if they can bring something or call to say that they'll be late or whatever. And when she knows that someone is coming, she cleans up her act enough that I look like some kind of alarmist who can't tell fact from fiction. If all you had to go on was what you saw when you came up and had lunch with her last month, would you have suspected anything was going on like what you saw there today?"

"No, I suppose not."

"See? That's what I'm up against. My dad's crazy and my mother is turning into a lush, and everyone thinks I'm the one who's losing her grip. My brother BJ might just as well be on another planet, but Darren and Maggie get up here pretty often, and Christine makes it at least three or four times a year, but what they see when they're here isn't what I see day in and day out. They've seen how out of it Daddy is, and they're worried about Mother, but mostly because of what they picture it must be like for her to deal with him every day."

"Well, don't you think it's exhausting to spend every waking minute with someone who can't remember what you call that thing that goes between your foot and your shoe?"

"Of course, Kate. If I spend one afternoon alone with my dad, I'm ready to slit my wrists. But what I'm afraid of is that she'll pass out—either from pills or liquor—and with no one there to watch him, he'll wander off into the woods, or worse, get in the car and be halfway to Kansas City before anyone knows he's gone."

Casey made the final turn and pulled up in the parking lot at Frank's Landscape and Nursery. The gravel crunched underneath the tires as she drew up next to Kate's Volvo. The two sat quietly for a moment.

"Forgive me for changing the subject, but why did your mother keep calling you Karen today?"

"Oh, gawd," Casey snorted, "I've tried for most of my life to get free of that. I'm surprised that you've known my mother for as long as you have and don't know my real name. When she's had a little too much happy juice, she starts using it again."

"Real name?"

"Yes, Mother was in one of her deep southern moods when I was born. My given name is Kayrun—spelled K-A-Y-R-U-N—Clarice, accent on the second syllable. That's what they called me when I was little. I hated it—at first because it sounded like a hillbilly name and then later because it sounded so dramatic, like some kind of tragic Faulkner heroine or something. When I left home to go to college, I started using my initials, KC. Somehow that mutated into Casey. I've always felt like that suited me better than Kayrun Clarice. Don't you?"

"Oh, Kayrun Clarice, you do go on!" Kate chortled in her heaviest fake southern accent. "Maybe you should have it stenciled on the door of this little red chariot." Kate patted the armrest of the Nissan for emphasis.

"Oh, right. The perfect accompaniment to the bags of cow manure I haul around when I'm out on a job. Oh, by the way, I call this the moo mobile in honor of the piles of fertilizer I've lugged around in the load bed . . ."

"Kayrun Clarice and her moo mobile. I think it has potential. Probably better than Casey's crap wagon." For the first time in hours, both women allowed themselves the luxury of a laugh. They relaxed against the firm vinyl seat and let the vanishing sunlight work its magic, fading and dimming the hues and colors all around them. The nursery had closed at four; theirs were the only two vehicles remaining in the lot.

"I really appreciate your spending the day here, Kate." Casey reached to switch off the ignition, then stopped herself as a thought hit her. "Hey, I promised to buy you dinner to say thanks. What's your favorite kind of food?"

"Gee, Casey. It's already almost five," Kate demurred as she checked her watch in the twilight. "I've got a two-hour drive to get back to Atlanta, and frankly, my head is still just pounding. I don't think I'm up for dinner tonight. Maybe some other time?"

"You're sure you can't stay?" Casey glanced at Kate, who shook her head. "Well, next time we'll plan the day better," Casey promised. "You will come up again, won't you, Kate?" She knew she sounded too eager, but she couldn't help herself.

"I will. Do you think your mother will be upset about today? I mean about my having seen her—you know—with her guard down and all?"

"Chances are she won't remember a whole lot about what went on today. Sometimes I think she's having as many problems with her memory as Daddy is, only for different reasons, of course."

"You know, it's funny, Casey, I guess you and I are much closer in age than your mother and I are, but because she and I worked together all those years when I was just starting my career, I've always thought of her as my contemporary. I honestly think that today was the first time it's registered with me that she's probably twenty-five years older than me."

"She was sixty-one on her last birthday."

"Wow, and what are you, Casey? Thirty-five?"

"I'll be thirty-nine."

"No joke? You look great. Must be all that time in the clean mountain air."

"What about you, Kate?"

"I don't get much time in the clean mountain air."

"No, seriously, how old are you?"

"I just pushed past my forty-sixth mile marker in August."

"Huh. Well, she's not quite old enough to be your mother, but almost. Now that you mention it, I didn't think about the age thing either; you were just my mother's friend from work. And here, all the time, we're the ones who should have been hanging out together."

"Well, it's never too late, Casey. Except for today, that is. It *is* late and I've got to get on back down the road before I turn into a pumpkin."

"I hate to see you go."

Kate canted in her seat so that she had a better view of Casey's profile, now just a silhouette in the last gray light of the day.

"It's not like I unlocked the door to a happy ending for this mess with your parents, Casey."

"No, but now I know that there's at least one person in the world who doesn't think I'm making up wild stories about what's going on in the hills of Delano, North Carolina."

"I guess that's worth something."

"It's worth a lot." Casey swung her head so that she and Kate were face to face. "More than you know, Kate." Suddenly, Casey leaned across the seat, awkwardly arching over the floor-mount gearshift, and wrapped her arms around Kate's shoulders.

Ever so briefly, Kate draped her right arm across Casey's left shoulder and returned the embrace. "I've got to go," she said abruptly, extracting herself from Casey's arms. In one fluid motion, she lifted the door handle and got out of the truck. "Call me sometime and let me know how things are going," she tossed over her shoulder as she closed the door.

In a flash, Kate was in the Volvo and had the engine running. As Kate raised her hand in a farewell wave, Casey caught sight of the navy blue sweatshirt that she had loaned Kate earlier in the day. Casey pumped the crank and lowered the window, but before she could utter a word, Kate backed out and was gone.

"Wonder if I'll ever see that sweatshirt again?" Casey mused. "The hell with the sweatshirt. Will I ever see Kate Bingham again?"

Chapter 6

Katharine Lorraine Bingham was one of those people blessed with an unfailing sense of direction. Once she had been to a place, she could find her way back there and home again, day or night. After leaving Casey in the parking lot, she negotiated the turns and twists of the unlit back roads, wending her way back to the divided four-lane highway that would lead her back to Atlanta. The Volvo responded smoothly as she worked the five-speed engine. She reached over and punched the button to engage the CD player. Streisand's voice, smooth as mercury on glass, filled the car.

The distraction Kate was hoping for from Barbra's dulcet tones didn't come. Too many ghosts had been brought out of hiding in the course of the day, each bringing with it a host of memories, vying for attention.

Burr Marsden was well on his way to losing his mind. Watching him labor through the day, struggling to remember how to do routine things like use a fork or turn on a light and straining to come up with what names to use when referring to his wife and children was almost more than she could bear. Although her own father had been dead for more than six years, she was never more than a fleeting reminder away from reliving the horror of watching him die, synapse by synapse, as his brain rotted from the inside out. By the time it was done, he had forgotten how to do every single thing that constituted living. In the end, he finally forgot how to swallow and how to breathe and how to keep his heart beating. He died in a nursing home, tied to a bed, drowned in his own saliva.

When Ray Bingham died, Kate consoled herself with the notion that she would never have to face anything so wrenching again in her life. Her mother had died years earlier, while Kate was in college. It was a shock—pancreatic cancer that went through her like wildfire—but Kate was young then, more resilient. It was, of course, not just a case of Kate being pliant and youthful. Her mother had suspected that Kate was a lesbian and made it clear that she didn't approve. Both of Kate's sisters stood firmly in their mother's camp—queer just didn't cut it. Kate's father never said anything one way or the other about the subject. All he knew was that she was his baby, his darling, and he loved her fiercely—right up until the day he didn't recognize her anymore when she came through the door. After the funeral back in Wisconsin, Kate returned to New Haven, grateful to put the dead to rest and to get on with her life.

Kate could have spent the duration of the drive reflecting on what had happened to her own father and the similarities to what she suspected might lie ahead for Burr and his family, but a phrase from one of the songs on the CD player edged its way into her consciousness:

"Memories light the corners of my mind . . ." As though some unseen hand had snatched the remote control, the screen in Kate's mind flipped to another time and place.

Nikki Irving. Now there was a memory she could have done without.

✂✧

26

"Good morning. I'm Kate Bingham with the accounting firm of DeWitt, Scroggins, and Howell. I have power of attorney for Mr. and Mrs. Charles Voight."

"Nikki Irving, Internal Revenue Service." She flashed her credentials identifying herself as an auditor with the IRS. Kate was too busy being dazzled by the smile Nikki simultaneously flashed to pay much attention to the pocket commission. "Have a seat."

The home office of DeWitt, Scroggins, and Howell, housed in the heart of Atlanta, had hired Kate directly out of college. They put her to work as an account representative handling individuals with annual adjusted gross incomes under a hundred thousand dollars. In her first year with the firm, she spent a lot of time at the Federal Building in downtown Atlanta meeting with assorted IRS agents, defending deductions, explaining the reasons she believed expenses were work-related, and generally showing off her knowledge of tax regulations. In most of those meetings, Kate was the one in control, even though she always tried to let the IRS auditors think that they were running the show. That morning, almost a quarter century ago, trapped in the aura of Nikki Irving's charm, she was a bumbling incompetent. She stammered and stuttered, she lost her train of thought, she buckled on issues she usually fought to the death over. When it was over, the Voights had a bill for additional tax due and Kate had a bad case of "gotta-see-her-again-itis."

Kate knew better than to do anything that could even smack of impropriety or conflict of interest, so she waited until the Voights' account had been settled and then asked that it be reassigned to another representative at DeWitt, Scroggins, and Howell. Before turning the records over to the new representative, Kate carefully copied down the phone number that was on Nikki's business card stapled to the inside of the file folder.

Two days later, with sweating palms and a racing heart, she placed the call.

"Internal Revenue, Nikki Irving, can I help you?"

"I hope so." And then her brain went numb.

"Hello? Can I help you?"

Kate fumbled for a coherent sentence. "Nikki, it's Kate Bingham. I met with you a couple of months ago on a tax audit." She gulped. "Voight. Mr. and Mrs. Charles Voight."

"Sure, I remember. Business expense adjustments and some disallowed charitable contributions. Additional tax due, with interest, no penalties. I thought I closed that out as a full pay a week or two ago. Is there a problem?"

"No. Well, yes. I mean, not with the Voights' audit. Oh hell, this was a mistake. I'm sorry to have bothered you."

Nikki stopped her before she could hang up. "Kate, wait. I'm glad to hear from you." Kate could picture that million-dollar smile beaming across the phone line. "What's on your mind?"

With uncharacteristic bravado, Kate replied simply, "You."

"Pardon?"

"*You* are on my mind. And you have been since the day I met you at the Voights' audit. I fall asleep thinking of you and wake up thinking of you. And if you report me to my boss, well, that's just the way it goes."

"Report you for what? Doing what I've been wishing I had the guts to do?" There was a break in the dialog. "Look, this fishbowl that I work in isn't exactly a good place to have a conversation. Can I meet you someplace after work today?"

And so it started. Within four months, Nikki Irving had moved in with Kate Bingham.

Kate's account assistant, Nora Marsden, had been invaluable in helping Kate learn the ropes at DS & H. Nora was not only technically savvy, she was a whiz at steering a course through the political morass at the anally-retentive accounting firm.

"So, are you liking Atlanta, Kate?" Nora inquired innocently one morning while the two of them were alone in the reference library researching a case.

"Sure. What's not to like?"

"Mind if I offer an observation?"

"I guess not."

"I'm the mother of five children; they always think that they can keep a secret from me, but they can't. I can always tell when something is going on in their lives, good or bad."

"And so . . . ?"

"And so, if I were a betting woman, I'd lay money that you've fallen in love since coming to town."

"What makes you say that, Nora?"

"Just humor me, Kate. Am I right or not?"

"Well . . ." Kate's face lit up just thinking about the notion of being in love with Nikki Irving.

"But I also bet it's not the sort of thing you'd like plastered on a billboard." Kate's countenance fell, despite her efforts to keep a poker face.

"I don't need details, Kate. And let me tell you right off, I don't care in the least about the gender of the lucky person you're keeping company with, but you've got to know that the prune-faced old farts who run this accounting firm don't exactly have a long track record of open-mindedness."

"What should I do, Nora?"

"For the most part, what you've been doing. Come to work every day, work your cases, keep your nose clean, don't rock the boat. When all the dust clears, all they really care about is the bottom line. Don't embarrass the partners, don't embarrass the clients, and don't give them any ammunition to use against you."

"Do you think many people here know—um—about me, Nora?"

"Nah, they're too busy cramming their noses up the big guys' butts to notice anything but their own career tracks and bonus tallies. I just would hate to see a promising young thing like you have her future get derailed for something that's really nobody's business."

So, on Nora's advice, Kate and Nikki played the games—two phone lines at the apartment, separate checking accounts, individual titles on vehicles, limited calls to one another at respective places of business, no pictures of each other at their workstations, avoiding references to "we" when speaking of weekend or evening activities in conversations with coworkers. Neither liked the charade, but both liked their paychecks.

With one parent dead and two sisters who had written her off as worthless, Kate found in Nikki the family she thought she'd never have. Nikki's parents and only brother lived in the Atlanta area. They seemed blissfully unconcerned about the fact that Nikki spent all of her time with another unmarried woman. One year led to two, two to two more, and in what felt like the blink of an eye, Kate and Nikki had been together for a decade.

When DeWitt, Scroggins, and Howell offered Kate a promotion if she moved to Chicago, Nikki worked out a transfer for herself so that they could relocate—in separate moving vans—together. From Chicago, they went to Detroit, and then from there to New Haven. While they were in New Haven, Kate's dad died. In deference to her sisters' outright disdain for Nikki, Kate braved the funeral alone.

They had been through so much together—eighteen years of whatever life had flung their way. The inch-by-inch death of her father had exhausted Kate, but now that that horrific chapter was closed, Kate looked forward to spending the rest of her life in peace with Nikki. She was confident that she and Nikki would always be a team. From the start, they called one another The Oddity and The Countess, the auditor and the accountant. But then one day, two years after Ray Bingham died, Nikki called it quits.

If there had been signs along the way, Kate had been oblivious to them. Nothing had changed, as far as she could tell. According to Nikki, that was precisely the problem.

"I can't do this anymore, Kate. I can't go on living this dull, predictable life. I'm so sick of you I could scream." And within a month of making that statement, Nikki packed up and left.

Kate only knew one way to approach a problem. If it couldn't be solved by reason and logic, it couldn't be solved. It had been four years since Nikki left, and she was no closer to knowing why than she had been on the day the door slammed. She had resigned herself to the probability that she would wonder till her dying day what she had done to make Nikki fall out of love with her.

The hundred-plus miles between Delano and Atlanta had vanished while Kate relived the two biggest, blinding hurts of her life. She exited off I-85 onto Lennox Road and covered the last few blocks home. She used the remote control to raise the security gate for the parking ramp access to her condo building and guided the Volvo into its assigned spot. She locked the car and activated its security system before walking over to the glass-enclosed lobby. With her keycard pass, she summoned the elevator and rode up to the fourteenth floor.

Once inside, she poured herself a glass of wine and flipped on the television. She wandered back to the bedroom to undress and to find more aspirin for her throbbing head. As she pulled off Casey Marsden's navy blue sweatshirt, she was struck by the fragrance that wafted up from it—something of a cross between newly turned earth and an evocative musk. She wondered at the vaguely familiar stirrings that rose unbidden somewhere deep within her as the memory of Casey's arms around her forced itself to mind.

"Katharine Lorraine Bingham, you are such an idiot," she blurted aloud to the empty room. "It only took you half a lifetime to figure out how Nora Marsden knew you were a lesbian."

Kate thought about all of the signposts along the way that she had simply failed to let register. She realized that, through the years, anytime Casey was present when Kate was visiting Nora, Nora had all but illuminated a neon arrow over Casey's head saying "Here's my lesbian daughter," but Kate was so caught up in protecting herself (and Nikki), she had blithely sailed right past it.

That night, with Nora's lesbian daughter's sweatshirt as a pillow, Kate lay down on her bed and cried for all that had been and for all that was yet to come.

31

Chapter 7

"Here, you might need this today." Unannounced and uninvited, Kate drove up to Delano the following Saturday and went directly to Frank's Landscape and Nursery. She wandered in and out of the various buildings among the remaining fall plants and potted trees until she found Casey in one of the greenhouses. "Thanks for the loan." She offered the washed and folded navy blue sweatshirt to Casey.

"The way they've got me running, I'll probably have to strip naked before the day is done." Casey smiled warmly as she took the shirt from Kate. "It's our last weekend before we close for the winter months. Hard to believe it's the end of October already." Her voice dropped half an octave. "I'm kinda surprised to see you, Kate. I was afraid I'd chased you off for good after last weekend."

"Obviously not. Here I am—complete with my own appropriate attire." She made a show of modeling her sea foam green sweatshirt with black lettering saying "Bah Hahbah." Underneath, in smaller letters, it read, "Translation for tourists, 'Bar Harbor.'" She scanned the nearly empty racks in the greenhouse. "Good thing you're closing for the season. There's not enough left here to do the flower boxes at the front door to my condo building."

"Frank's pretty good at guessing how much to order. We ran a big sale over the past week and moved out a lot of stuff. Sometimes, at the end of the season, he has to take a truckload down to a dealer in Florida, but I don't think there's enough to justify that this year." She finished stacking the plastic pots on the table in front of her and gave the open room a sweeping glance. "I'm about done in here. Want to go with me out to the overflow yard? I need to dig up a bunch of small fruit trees and put them in buckets. We'll store them inside for the next couple of months to protect them from the heavy frost."

Casey draped the sweatshirt around her shoulders and grabbed a shovel and a stack of large containers from the corner near the door. Kate followed her outside. "We'll take the moo mobile. I can just load them in the backend and bring them up when I'm done." The two women walked the short distance to the Nissan. Casey tossed the tools in the load bed and they got in the cab. Beyond the storage building with the loading dock, there was a narrow, grassy lane that wound around back into the woods. A quarter mile down the trail, they emerged on an open plot of ground lined with rows of cultivated trees ranging in height from two feet to twenty.

"I had no idea this was back here," Kate observed as they pulled to a stop.

"All together, Frank has almost thirty acres of land that he uses for this nursery. There are holding beds and tree yards tucked all over out here." Casey gestured expansively. She opened her door but hesitated before getting out. "Is my mother expecting you today, Kate?" She looked back toward the passenger seat.

"Only if she has ESP. I didn't tell her I was coming, if that's what you mean."

"Well, it's just that I didn't know that you were coming, either, so I was just wondering . . ."

Kate exhaled forcefully through her nostrils. "I suppose I should have called first, shouldn't I?" She looked down at her hands in her lap. "What say we get busy digging up these trees and I'll try to make up for my rudeness? Do you have a pair of gloves I can borrow?"

"Not rude, just a surprise. And sure. There's at least half a dozen pairs under the seat."

Both women exited the truck and stood inside their respective cocked doors. Kate rummaged under her side of the vinyl bench and came up with one left blue glove and one brown right glove. "Never let it be said I don't strive to make a fashion statement," she said with a flourish as she pulled the gloves on.

They closed the doors and walked around to the rear of the truck. Casey dropped the load gate and tugged the shovel out.

"Here, I'll take the pots," Kate offered.

"Thanks. We only have to get the little guys. The rest of them will make it through the winter on their own." They set off toward the row of shortest trees.

"What are these anyway, Casey? The bark is so pretty."

"They're Kwanzan cherry trees. Ornamental. They have those really pretty cluster blooms of tight pink flowers in the spring. Then they make a mess of your yard when the blooms fall off."

"Oh, yeah, I remember seeing them around town. Where but America would we have fruit trees that don't bear fruit?"

Casey jammed the blade of the shovel into the dirt around the base of one of the trees. "Well, these are native to Japan, so I guess we're not the only ones who do things just for show."

As Casey loosened the soil around the tree, Kate grasped the trunk and lifted it from the hole. She dropped the root ball into one of the pots and used her hands to scoop more dirt into the container. "One," she intoned as she set it aside.

"You accountants always have to count everything don't you? Didn't they name a character after you on *Sesame Street*?" Casey giggled as she moved to the next tree. "Oh, wait. I guess that would be 'Countess' in your case."

Kate was momentarily stunned at hearing the term of endearment that Nikki used to use for her. She sucked up her courage and replied, "You know, there used to be someone in my life who called me that."

"Yeah?"

"Uh-huh. Did your mother ever mention Nikki Irving to you?"

Casey stopped digging and rested her chin on the end of the shovel. Her eyes were on a level plane with Kate's.

"She was your lover."

"Right." Kate wanted to correct her and say, "And best friend, and partner, and soul mate, and hope, and reason, and haven, and family, and if I'm really lucky, I can go three days in a row without missing her," but instead she just twisted her mouth in a wry grin and added, "Was."

Casey returned her attention to the Kwanzan tree. "So what happened?"

"If you ever find Nikki Irving, you have my permission to try to find out."

"What does that mean?"

"It means that I can't tell you what I don't know. She left. One day just over four years ago, she took her things and moved out. I've only heard from her once since then and that was to tell me that her grandmother had passed away. There wasn't even a return address on the envelope." Kate lifted the second tree and placed it in a pot. "Next question?" She clapped the dirt from her gloves.

"Is that why you came back to Atlanta?"

Kate furrowed her brow. "I suppose so. I haven't really done much thinking since Nikki left. I sort of went on autopilot and let life take me where it would. Early this year, DS and H made an offer for me to come back here, and I said, 'Why not?' At least the climate is better."

"You know that Mother always held you up to me as the example of what I could be."

"A lonely, middle-aged workaholic?"

Casey laughed in spite of herself. "Well, let's turn the calendar back a few years. I didn't exactly have an easy time coming to terms with my sexual identity. It's kind of ironic. Most kids have to fight like the devil to get their parents to accept that they're gay. In my case, I think they had an easier time of it than I did. Mother would encourage me by pointing out how well you were doing at Dewey, Screwum, and Howe. And every year when your Christmas card to her would come, she'd comment about how long you and Nikki had been together."

"And what did she say the year the card came telling her that we weren't together anymore?" Kate asked.

"Huh." Casey's response was half laugh, half grunt. "It wouldn't have mattered what she said. I doubt that I'd have heard it."

"Oh? Why is that?"

"It was the same year I lost Lindsay."

"Lindsay?"

"My lover. We had been together for eight years."

"She took a hike, too?"

Casey paused again in her labors. "The longest possible one." Her voice cracked. "She had breast cancer. She gave it a real battle, but in the end, it was stronger than she was." Casey flicked a tear from her cheek. "Thought it was going to kill me, too, but it looks like I'm still here."

Kate released her hold on the reed-thin tree and took two steps toward Casey. She held out her arms and Casey folded into them. "I'm sorry." She waited for further inspiration, but none came. "I don't know what else to say." She lifted her right hand and pressed Casey's head against her shoulder.

Casey burrowed deeply into Kate's embrace. "Every time I think I'm past it and that I can talk about it without falling apart, I prove myself a liar." She sniffed and swallowed hard. "You'd think four years would be enough."

"Take it from one who knows. Four years is hardly a minute on the clock that keeps time when you're healing from a broken heart." Kate felt tears stinging the backs of her eyelids. She wrapped her arms all the more tightly around Casey.

Locked in the circle of one another's arms, they stood in the gentle noontime sun, grateful for the warmth—from it and from each other.

Kate loosened her grip on Casey and cupped her hands on Casey's shoulders as the two women disentangled. For the first time, she let herself really look into Casey's bottomless blue eyes. She felt them searching her own in return. "So tell me about Lindsay," she offered as she dropped her hands by her side.

"What do you want to know?" Casey leaned over and retrieved the shovel from where it had fallen several minutes earlier.

"What did you love most about her?"

"That she loved me." She sank the shovel into the earth.

"Where did you meet?"

"I never really tended bar in the Underground. I just used that as my cover story. I was the bartender at Garbo's, the woman's bar over on Cheshire Bridge. She'd come in on my nights to work and order about twenty club sodas in the course of an evening. I figured she either had the hots for me or was an undiagnosed diabetic. By the way, I always expected I'd see you there one night."

"Nikki and I didn't hit the bars much. We stayed pretty close to the closet." Kate waited a few seconds before continuing. "Had you been involved with anyone before her?"

"Oh, sure. One amateur romp with a girl in high school, the usual sweating up the sheets stuff with assorted jocks down at Florida State, and a couple of short-lived flings with women I met at softball and with the other bartenders. Things like that."

"But Lindsay was different?"

Casey paused with the shovel in midair. "Yeah. Different. With any of the others, the morning after, I'd be making up reasons to get away from them as fast as I could, but the first night with her, I remember thinking, 'so this is what all those sappy love songs on the radio are about.' I hated to leave her, even if I knew I'd see her again in a couple of hours. Every time I saw her, even up till the day she died, I'd get this rush. It was a flood of happiness, just seeing her face. She was the most beautiful woman I've ever known."

"Has there been anyone since?"

"No," Casey replied softly. "It felt like I'd be cheating on her." She pitched another shovelful of dirt. "I guess that sounds pretty stupid, huh?"

"Not at all. I don't think we stop loving somebody just because they died."

"Or just because they went away?"

"Touché," Kate answered with a wan smile. "Or just because they went away."

They worked on in silence for a while, Casey freeing the trees from the ground, Kate putting them in the pots and adding more soil as necessary.

"So why are you here today, Kate?"

"I had to make an honest woman of myself and return your sweatshirt."

Casey laughed lightly. "A two-hundred-mile roundtrip to return a stained, used sweatshirt? Seems like a lot of work." She looked over the remaining trees in the field. "That should do it. The others are big enough to survive the winter." She laid the shovel down and took off her gloves. She reached a hand up and ran her fingers through her hair, then rolled her head from side to side and arched her shoulders. "Ready to load these bad boys up and get them back to the greenhouse?" Casey bent as if to hoist one of the containers of trees, but Kate caught her by the upper arm before she could pick it up.

Wordlessly, she turned Casey a quarter turn so that they were standing face to face, then drew her to her body. Ever so gently, she laid her lips on Casey's, not sure if the kiss would be returned or rejected. Casey pulled back and studied Kate's face. Whatever she saw there was enough; whatever sign she needed was provided. She pressed in tight against Kate and kissed her with a passion that she had been sure would never be granted to her again.

And when Kate returned that passion in kind, they both knew that the clocks inside their broken hearts could finally start marking the passing of time.

Chapter 8

"You got away last time without letting me buy you dinner. I'm not letting that happen again."

The sun was sliding down behind the hills on the far side of the main building at Frank's Landscape and Nursery. Kate and Casey had worked side by side all afternoon getting the place ready for the off-season. Casey would work a few hours a day for the next week or two to take care of any loose ends, but the worst of it had been accomplished.

After the kiss they exchanged out by the cherry trees, they had found every possible excuse to make physical contact with each other. "Here, let me help you up." "I need to get that rake behind you." "Look at the intricate vein pattern in this leaf." A hand on a shoulder. Hands clasped just a moment longer than necessary when pulling each other up from a bench or the ground. Leaning in close when arm's length would have sufficed. A palm laid gently in the small of the back when one passed behind the other.

"Look at me. I'm a dirty mess. I don't think there's a restaurant in the county that would let me in." Kate didn't look all that bad, but Casey let the remark pass.

"Who said I was willing to be seen in public with you, little Ms. Bah Humbug?" Casey teased. "Let's get Chinese and take it to my place. Or if you don't like Chinese, then barbecue or whatever you want."

"For the tenth time, it's Bar Harbor." Kate pointed to the lettering on her sweatshirt. "And Chinese is fine, Casey. Gosh, all of a sudden, I'm starving."

"Well, we didn't get lunch, so that's not really a surprise."

"Follow me into town and we'll grab dinner. Then I'll take you to the house."

Delano was a quick drive from Frank's nursery. They popped into the Many Fortunes restaurant in the strip mall on the edge of town and placed their order. Three small, mismatched dinette chairs with plastic covers on the seat cushions were lined up across from the front counter. They claimed two of them and sat next to one another while the cook prepared their kung pao chicken, shrimp foo young, and Buddha's Delight vegetable dish. The outsides of their thighs touched, lightly at first, then with more pressure as the minutes passed. By the time the waiter brought the brown bag containing their order, it was all either of them could do to keep her hands to herself.

"Think that Swedish meatball can keep up with the moo mobile once we start to climb some serious hills?" Casey asked as they opened doors to their respective vehicles.

"You'll be lucky if I don't pass you on the first curve," Kate retorted, grinning.

"It's left out of here, right at the light, then about six miles down the road. We only have to make two turns once we leave the highway. The first road will be paved, but the road up to the house is gravel. It gets pretty steep toward the end."

"Not to worry. I'll be right behind you."

Twilight had turned to dusk and dusk to night. Kate tracked closely behind Casey, trying to concentrate on the roads, but it was a fool's errand. The only thing on her mind was the woman behind the wheel of the red Nissan in front of her.

For her part, Casey kept checking the rearview mirror, ostensibly to be sure that she hadn't lost Kate, but the real reason was to reassure herself that this wasn't just a fantasy. Kate Bingham—*the* Kate Bingham whom she had revered and marveled at and adored (from afar, of course) for longer than she could recall—was on her way to Casey's house. The excitement was almost more than she could contain. Only once did she falter. "Lindsay, honey," she whispered to the night air as she rounded the final corner, "if you were still with me, I'd never even consider this. I miss you, baby. I hope you understand."

Casey wheeled into the yard and parked near the front door. She hopped out of the pickup and motioned for Kate to pull under the carport off to the right of the house. "Frost will set early tonight," she explained. "If you're under there, your windows won't get all covered over."

Kate parked and joined Casey as she stretched back into the pickup and turned off the engine. A small dusk-till-dawn halogen lamp mounted on a tall pole lit the way from the carport to the house. "You weren't kidding when you said we'd climb a little to get here. I had to drop all the way down to second on that last incline."

"Yeah, it's almost high enough to cause a nosebleed. Here, you take this," Casey directed, handing the brown bag of square containers from Many Fortunes to Kate. "Roger is going to come out of the door like a bullet, and I better have both hands free to corral him."

"The dog, I take it?"

"Right. He'll settle down in a just a minute or two, but he's been inside all day, so you'll have to excuse his exuberance."

Casey slipped the key in the lock and opened the door. Right on cue, a small brown-and-white dog bolted out the door and dashed around the yard like he was possessed by a demon. He took time out

41

to relieve his bladder, then charged back and forth between Casey and Kate a dozen times. "Go on inside, Kate. I'll wait out here for him to come to his senses." Casey reached around the doorjamb and flipped on the entryway light and the light above the front door. "Wander around and make yourself at home. I'll just be a couple of minutes."

Kate stepped in the door and set the bag on the table just inside and to the left. She turned on the table lamp and glanced around the room. Without realizing it, she had expected Casey's house to be like Nora's, with traditional furnishings and a country kitchen atmosphere. She missed it by a mile. The great room was a study in Danish modern. The coffee table, the bookcases, the entertainment center, the end tables, the dining table and hutch were all light teak. The sofa and the two armchairs were a light gray fabric with teak legs and trim. The rugs on the hardwood floor were done in muted tones of rose and green and gray. The pictures on the wall—what she could see of them in the diffused light from the table lamp and the overhead light in the entryway—were simple line drawings matted in thin black metal frames, depicting women doing everything from walking hand in hand to dancing to making love. Several small statues and art pieces sat on the surfaces around the room. They all appeared to be soft and round with graceful, soothing edges. Some were made of wood, others of marble or other stone, one of porcelain. Kate walked over to the entertainment center and lifted one of the wooden ones from its place near the CD player. It seemed to fit perfectly in her hands. She was holding it—all but caressing it—as Casey and Roger came through the front door.

"Everyone is always drawn to that one first. Careful there, Kate, she's a New Guinea fertility goddess."

"Well, watch for that star in the east," Kate cackled as she replaced it on the shelf. "What a pretty room, Casey."

"Thanks. Maybe not what most people would regard as appropriate for a cabin in the woods, but it suits me." Casey dropped onto a footstool near the door and began untying her shoelaces.

"I guess I had anticipated Queen Anne with chintz and some Grant Woods prints."

"No, you have me confused with my mother. If I see one more chair upholstered with a multi-colored tea rose print, I'll gag." Casey was using one hand to cuff the dog as he nudged her feet and ankles while working at a knot in her shoestring with the other.

"I thought your parents' house looked really nice."

"Yeah, I guess, if you like to perch on the edge of a chair and point your pinky finger." Casey finished removing her shoes and rose to her feet. "Have the cats made an appearance yet?"

"Not that I've noticed."

"They're probably in the bedroom. Come on back and I'll show you the rest of the place." Casey led the way down the hallway that ran off the right side of the great room. She hit the light switch at the end of the hall. "This is the guest bath." She gestured to the room on the left. "Here's the second bedroom," she gestured to her right to the doorway on the other side of the hall, "and this is the mistress bedroom. 'Master' is just too sexist, don't you think?" They stepped into a large room that spanned the depth of the house, front to rear. "Kitty kids," she called, "are you in here?" She pulled the chain on a floor lamp standing just inside the doorway.

Curled together on the queen-sized bed were two smallish cats, one mostly black except for a white bib under her chin and an orange-and-white tiger-striped tabby with a splash of white across her nose.

"This is Caboodle," Casey said as she picked up the tabby. "That's Kit, doing her impersonation of an inside-out S." The tabby seemed accustomed to being held and cuddled and offered no resistance as Casey nuzzled her to her neck. The black cat yawned and stretched out to what looked twice her usual length, then contorted herself in more directions than one might think a cat could turn and still stay connected. A greatly calmed Roger had padded down the hall behind them and sat just inside the door wagging his tail.

"Caboodle and Kit," Kate repeated.

"Say it the other way around," Casey directed.

"Kit and Caboodle," Kate complied. "Oh, gawd, Casey. How could you?"

"Seemed like a good idea at the time."

Kate looked around the bedroom. Like the great room, it could have appeared on the cover of the Scan store's fall sale catalog. Centered on the far right wall, the mattress sat on a teak platform with a bookcase headboard. A teak rocker with a padded seat cushion angled across one corner. A sleek highboy occupied the corner opposite and a matching double dresser was on the wall opposite from where they were standing, flanked by a window on either side. The artwork on the walls was more dramatic than what she had seen in the great room. There were two bold abstract paintings done primarily in mauve and teal. The smaller one hung over the highboy and the larger one directly across from the doorway. There were three Georgia O'Keeffe prints hanging above the bed—one of a single deep purple pansy, one that looked like a white morning glory surrounded by green tones, and one that was a single oak leaf done in rusts and reds. To the left was a doorway in the center of the wall, which Kate surmised, led to a walk-in closet and bathroom. The room felt clean and airy, yet inviting and cozy.

"You're wasting your time at the nursery, Casey. You should have been an interior decorator."

"My parents would be happy to hear you say that. It's what I studied for two years when I couldn't make up my mind about what to major in. I'm sure they felt like they just threw all that money down a hole."

"Not at all. This place is beautiful." Kate looked appreciatively around the room again. "You own this house, right?"

"No, the bank owns it. Every month I offer a token of my gratitude to them for letting me live here in the form of a mortgage payment. Want to see the kitchen?" She gently dropped Caboodle back onto the bed.

"Sure."

Casey took them back down the hall and across the great room. Now that she had seen the entire house, Kate could see that it was laid out in three parts. The great room, positioned in the center of the house, occupied a little more than a third of the total space. The two bedrooms and baths lay to the right side of the great room, and the kitchen and combination mud room/utility room were to the left of the great room. It was readily evident that Casey hadn't had as much of a free hand in the kitchen's décor. The cabinets were an uninspired dark finish, the floor a mottled gray and brown vinyl, and the wallpaper a busy geometric pattern that clashed with the flooring.

"My least favorite room in the house," Casey commented as they entered and she switched on the lights. "One of these days, I'm going to give it a facelift." A double stainless steel sink with a window over it was in the middle of the counter that ran along the back wall. The refrigerator stood a few feet to the left, microwave slightly to the right, and a gas range was tucked in the corner. She took a few more steps forward. "Back there is the washer and dryer," she said as she pointed to the door ajar. "And the kitty boxes and the door to the back yard."

"Great house, Casey."

"Thanks. The kids and I like it." Roger had dutifully followed them to the kitchen. "Don't you, buddy?" Roger leaned into Casey and moaned a low acknowledgment as Casey squatted down and massaged his ears.

"So, do you want to shower before we eat?" Casey asked as she stood up. "I think I will."

"That might feel good. Maybe you've got a pair of sweatpants I could borrow to wear . . ."

"Of course. Let me grab that bag of food from the entryway and put it out of harm's way. If we leave it out, Roger will be searching for chopsticks the minute we hit the showers." Casey collected the bag from Many Fortunes and tucked it into the oven.

They walked back through the great room to the other side of the house. "You can use the hall bath while I shower in the back. Let me see what I've got clean that you can wear." Kate paused by the doorway to the bathroom while Casey continued to the bedroom. She was back shortly. "Here, this bright yellow will be great on you. I think I've only worn these once. My dorky sister gave me these for Christmas last year. It's the world's worst color for me—makes me look like I've got jaundice." Kate took the matching sweatshirt and pants from Casey. "There's a T-shirt, too, if you want it."

"Great. Thanks."

Their hands grazed momentarily as Kate took the clothing from Casey. They both were painfully aware that at long last, they were alone together in a private place. And neither had a clue about what to do next.

"Well, last one out is a rotten egg," Casey joked lamely. She turned and vanished into the far room.

Kate stepped into the bathroom and closed the door.She pulled the shower curtain back, reached into the tub, and opened the tap. She sat on the commode and took off her shoes, then stood and slipped out of her jeans and top. She was about to climb into the steaming stream coming from the showerhead when she realized that there wasn't a towel in sight. She looked under the vanity and cracked the door to see if she could spot a linen closet. No such luck.

"Casey?" she called. She could hear the shower running in the other bathroom. "Probably can't hear me," she muttered. She grabbed her Bar Harbor sweatshirt and held it to her chest as she tiptoed the short distance to the bedroom. She peeked around the doorframe, but all she saw was Kit and Caboodle dozing on the bed. "Casey?" she called again. No reply. "Must be a stack of towels somewhere," she hazarded. She took the few steps toward the door to the closet and bath and pushed the door slightly. All Kate could see was the empty shower stall with the water running, directly in front of the door.

Just then, Casey came out of the little room at the far end of the bathroom where the commode was housed. She gave a start at finding Kate in the doorway.

"Sorry. I didn't mean to scare you. I couldn't find a towel . . ."

Casey was standing less than three feet away from Kate, wearing exactly what she had been wearing the day she arrived on the planet. All of Kate's imaginings were made manifest. Casey looked every bit the goddess Diana—trim, fit, lean, muscular, and ready for the hunt.

What Kate hadn't realized is that she, too, had been startled by Casey's emergence from the lavatory and that she had dropped her hands from in front of her. She stood with her sweatshirt hanging in front of her knees.

"Uh, right over here," Casey said, barely above a whisper. She reached to her left, took a towel from the closet shelving, and extended it toward Kate.

At precisely the same instant, they both knew that there was no point fighting the feelings or pretending any longer. Kate let her shirt fall from her hands; Casey dropped the towel on the floor beside her. In a rush they were entwined around one another, touching, probing, kissing, grasping, thrusting, licking, sighing, feeling.

"Come on," Casey urged softly. She took Kate by the hand and led her into the shower stall. "It's OK. We've got plenty of towels."

Chapter 9

From the shower stall to the platform bed; from the bed to the floor with the down comforter as buffer from carpet burns; from the bedroom floor to the sofa in the great room; from the great room back to the bed. Roger and the cats politely removed themselves from room to room as the traveling lovefest made its way through the house.

Casey was lying on her back. Kate was lying next to her with her head in the concave of Casey's neck and shoulder. Casey's right arm lay lightly across Kate's back while Kate's left arm draped over Casey's rib cage.

"What does a girl have to do to get dinner in this place? You realize that it's nearly midnight, don't you?" From her vantage point, Kate could see the clock that sat on the far left side of the bookcase headboard.

"As they say down at the frog pond, 'Time's fun when you're

having flies,'" Casey replied, tightening her grip on Kate's body. "Are you trying to tell me you haven't enjoyed yourself?"

"Actually, I've been enjoying you," Kate murmured, turning her face up so that she could kiss Casey yet again, "but I need nourishment. For goodness' sake, I'm an old woman. You've put me through the equivalent of a marathon tonight. You can't expect me to survive without some sustenance."

"What a wimp, Bingham," Casey teased. "This was just a stroll in the park." She kissed Kate soulfully. "But I don't want to be accused of being insensitive. Besides, if you think this was a marathon, I've got plans to take you on a triathlon." She shifted her body. "Come on. I know this all-night Chinese place just the other side of the living room."

Casey swung her legs over the side of the bed and reached over to the rocker in the corner and picked up her bathrobe. She stood and slipped her arms into the holes and tied the powder blue terrycloth sash around her middle. She turned back to the bed to find Kate staring at her adoringly. She offered her right hand to Kate. "I don't think I've got another robe. Can you make do with that sweatsuit I gave you earlier?"

Kate took Casey's hand. With strength that surprised them both, she pulled Casey back down onto the bed. Casey caught herself on her knees and palms to avoid landing directly on top of Kate as she fell.

"Why should I have to be the one who struggles into pants and a shirt while you take the easy way out and wear the robe?" Kate raised up on her elbows so that she was inches away from Casey's face. She arched her neck so that she could reach Casey's lips. As they kissed, Casey slid down prone on top of Kate's body. Just before they melded together, Kate undid the sash on the robe and reached inside. As her hand found its way to Casey's breast, they both felt the surge of rekindled desire.

"Did you know," Kate whispered into Casey's ear, "that cold Chinese food for breakfast is supposed to be a great aphrodisiac?"

"Then we'd better stick with oatmeal," Casey rejoined as they resumed rocking rhythmically. "I'm not sure how much more arousal I can take."

Kate helped Casey work free of the robe and eased her onto her back. She started in the hollow of Casey's neck and began kissing her way down Casey's solid, supple form.

"Wait, Kate," Casey urged. "I don't want to be a spectator this time. Let's do this together."

The floor lamp by the doorway into the room had been on since Casey turned it on when she was first showing Kate the house. Its muted light was just enough for Kate to make out Casey's features in the shadows. Kate explored Casey's face seeking confirmation of her meaning.

"Here, I'll help you." She supported part of Kate's weight while Kate rotated above Casey's midsection. Kate lay back down carefully, feeling the heat from Casey's hands all but melting the backs of her thighs as she did so.

For all either of them knew, the clock on the headboard ceased keeping time and the earth skipped a rotation. Time and motion were suspended. All that existed anywhere in the universe was this single, unitized entity, an instrument vibrating in a harmonized pitch, moving toward the perfect coda. When the crescendo passed, the world had sense enough to sit silently by and wait respectfully before bestirring itself into moving forward.

"You are an amazing woman, Casey Marsden." Kate purred as she resettled herself on Casey's shoulder.

"Ditto your own self, Kate." They lay listening to one another breathe for a few moments. "Oh, and by the way, thanks for bringing my sweatshirt back. I guess I'm going to have to start loaning them out more regularly. This was a pretty good payback." She ran her hand up and down Kate's upper arm as she spoke.

"I have a suggestion."

"What's that?"

"If you feel a sudden urge to loan out one of your lousy stained sweatshirts, call me first. I want rights of first refusal."

"You mean you'd do this again, Kate?"

"Maybe once or twice more, if you're lucky."

"You mean tonight or over the rest of our lives?"

"I'm not saying; I think it's better to keep you guessing. After all, I don't want you to start taking me for granted."

"How about if I take you to the kitchen and we continue this conversation over a dinner of Kung Pao and petrified rice? Or maybe I should say over a very early breakfast. It's after one o'clock." Casey roused herself slightly.

"Oh sure, now that you're hungry, we can go eat. Seems like I made the same proposal a while ago and look what came of it."

"I know." Casey's voice came out low and husky. "I wanted to see if the offer had the same effect on you that it had on me."

Kate hesitated for only an instant. "Next time, we'd probably better get pizza."

Chapter 10

"You mean it's been almost five years since you've seen your sisters?" Casey paused as she worked her way through a second serving of vegetables and foo young.

At long last, they had managed to quench the initial fires of pent-up passion and were sitting side by side at the dining room table eating reheated Chinese food.

"Uh-huh. I went back to Wisconsin a couple of times in the year or so after Dad died to help take care of what was left of his belongings and to settle up medical bills and stuff like that. They both were such pains in the ass that I decided I was just trying to teach a pig to sing." Kate pulled the kung pao container nearer to her and dipped a spoonful onto her plate.

"What?"

"You know—never try to teach a pig to sing. It wastes your time and annoys the pig. It was obvious that they weren't going to suddenly accept my perverted lifestyle, so I just quit going back to the Midwest."

"But they're the only family you've got. Makes for kind of a lonely life, doesn't it, Kate?"

"Better lonely than feeling constantly judged and found lacking. Besides, at first, I still had Nikki . . ." Her voice trailed off.

"What did your sisters do when you told them that you and she had broken up?" Casey finished her meal and pushed her plate toward the center of the table.

"Ha. Like I'd waste long distance minutes or the price of a stamp sharing that news with either of them." Kate took a long drink of water. "It wouldn't surprise me if they thought we were still together."

"Don't you even remember each other's birthdays or do Christmas presents or anything?" Casey asked, incredulous.

"No presents. They usually just sign their names to a card. Maybe there's a line or two about what the kids are doing, but trust me, we are not going to be mistaken for the Lennon sisters." Kate took the last forkful from her plate and stacked it with Casey's on the table. "Enough about the Bingham bitches. Let's hear about the Marsden mob."

"Oh, I'm sure Mother filled you in with every little detail that day you and she had lunch. It's always a prime topic in her repertoire."

"No, not really. She hit the highlights, but your dad kept interrupting. We really talked more about her than we did about your brothers and sisters." Kate peeled the cellophane wrapper from a fortune cookie and broke it in two. "And then, of course, she and I made that ill-advised trip to Frank's Landscape and Nursery that afternoon." She gave a half laugh as she gazed intently at Casey. "Was she playing matchmaker?" She laid the uneaten cookie on her place mat.

"Oh, I doubt it. Mother adores you—like some kind of accounting icon—but I don't think she ever thought of you and me as likely candidates for hers and hers monogrammed towels." Casey squinted at Kate as she considered the possibility. "No," she continued with a shake of her head. "I think she just wanted to get away from Daddy for a while that day. I think one of the biggest issues is that she's real embarrassed by him—how he acts, I mean." Casey's face clouded over and she averted her eyes from Kate.

"What, babe?" Kate asked gently as she laid a palm alongside Casey's cheek and brought her face back to meet her own.

"She used to be so proud of him. She'd take his arm whenever they were around people, almost like she was saying, 'This one's mine, and isn't he fine?' When they'd have these huge parties at our house down in Atlanta, I'd hear her talking and she'd say, 'My husband—he's an engineer, you know—.' It was almost like it gave her an identity or something. Now, she's just the wife of a guy who can't remember that the button side of the shirt goes in the front."

"And what about you, Casey? This change in your dad can't be easy for you, either."

Casey jutted her chin toward the ceiling and contemplated her response. "You know what?" She pursed her lips. "I think I like him better this way." She lowered her chin. "Not crazy out of his mind— that's not what I mean. It's just that when we kids were growing up, my father was never home. He was always at the office working on some hotsy snotsy project. He missed all of the boys' ball games, all of my sisters' concerts, our birthday parties, confirmations, awards ceremonies, you name it. Half the time, he wasn't even home for holiday dinners. Or if he was there, he'd bolt down the meal and then go to his den and close the door." She emitted a small laugh. "We used to feel bad because he was never around. Now, he's here all the time, except, of course, he's still not really here." She took a breath and then added, "At least there's not all the yelling and screaming anymore."

"Yelling and screaming?" Kate queried.

"He was always so agitated about his work. Any little thing would send him into a rage. We all walked on eggshells any time he was at home."

"I guess I can see why you'd say the way he is now is a better option."

"Yeah, except Mother feels so cheated."

"Because . . ."

"Because she put up with all his crap all those years in hopes that they'd have this swell retirement. She had it all planned out that they'd have this ritzy house on Lake Lanier with a boat docked out back. And all their old friends from Atlanta would come to all their dress-up parties and she'd play bridge with her friends and go to art shows. And they'd travel and see all the things that always got put off in deference to his job. Hell, she's lucky if she sees the grocery store these days." She ticked off each item on her fingers as she spoke.

"Just goes to show we never can bank on the future, I guess."

"That's an understatement. Look at us." Casey ran her index finger around the rim of her water glass. "I sure never figured I'd be planting pansies in the hills of North Carolina. And I absolutely hadn't planned on being a babysitter for my parents—at least not so soon."

"I've been meaning to ask you about that. I thought you probably moved up here for that very reason."

"No. Not at all. After Lindsay died, I tried to pick up the pieces and get on with life, but everywhere I went in Atlanta just reminded me of her. I couldn't even stand to drive past Garbo's anymore, let alone tend bar there. I changed jobs about half a dozen times in the first two years after she died. I moved to a different apartment. I sold both of our cars and got an SUV. I even tried going to church for a while. Nothing helped."

"So?"

"So one weekend about two years after Lindsay died, I was up here to see my parents. Mother wanted to get some plants for a garden she was making. She was doing it all in flowers that bloomed in white—called it her meditation spot. We went driving around and stumbled on Frank's place. They had a Help Wanted sign in the window."

"You applied on the spot?"

"No, I came back up the following Monday. I didn't want my parents to know I was even considering it. For that matter, I wasn't sure I *was* considering it. It's a miracle Frank hired me. When he asked me what I knew about gardening, all I could tell him was the names of the things Mother had bought when we had been there two days earlier. He either was desperate for cheap help or he felt sorry for me. Either way, he offered me the job and I took it."

"Are you sorry you did?"

"No, not for a minute. I needed to do something really different or I'd never have survived." Casey heaved a sigh. "I suppose that sounds terribly dramatic." She flung the back of her hand to her forehead and tossed her head for effect.

"You're entitled, Casey. I know how hard it can be to watch someone you love die." Kate cleared her throat. "You still miss her, don't you?"

"Of course."

The clock on the bookshelf behind the table ticked off the minutes.

"Do you want to talk about it?" Kate prompted, not sure if she could bear the answer.

"Not really, Kate, but thanks for asking." Casey gave a half smile.

More minutes fell from the clock face.

"We'd better finish up here." Casey gestured to the nearly empty containers in front of them. "Do you want anything more?"

"Just this fortune cookie," Kate replied, retrieving it from the place mat. "Where's yours?"

"Right here." Casey pulled a still-wrapped cookie from the stack of soy sauce and hot mustard packets on the table. "What does yours say?"

Kate took the slip of paper from her broken cookie, but held it cupped in her closed hand. "Help. I'm being held prisoner in a Chinese bakery."

"Very funny. Really—what does it say?"

"You have to eat the cookie first or else it doesn't come true."

"Yeah?"

"Uh-huh. It's the rule." Kate popped a bite of cookie into her mouth.

"Well, no wonder I've had such lousy luck all my life. I've been reading the fortune before I ate the cookie."

"That's probably it." Kate finished off the rest of her cookie; Casey did the same.

"OK, now we can see what the Many Fortunes restaurant has to say about our futures," Kate directed. "You first."

Casey skimmed the tiny slip of paper. She looked up and met Kate's gaze. "Be ready to meet the love of your life." She extended the fortune to Kate. "What's yours?"

"A new romance will heal old wounds."

They hunted for reactions on one another's face.

"You know, Kate, it really wouldn't be right to ignore prophecy of 'ancient Chinese baker.'" Casey moved over in her chair so that she was within an inch of Kate. She cradled Kate's chin in her hand and drew her nearer. She leaned in and kissed Kate sweetly but fervently.

Casey pulled back from Kate and pushed her chair away from the table. "Help me stash this stuff." She waved at the cartons and dirty dishes.

Wordlessly, the two women swept the remnants of the meal from the table and took them to the kitchen. Casey tossed plates and silverware into the sink and rinsed them off while Kate threw empty containers in the trash or stacked those worth saving in the refrigerator.

"Now, where were we?" Casey whispered as she stepped up behind Kate and wrapped her arms around her waist.

"You're supposed to go out and meet someone and I'm supposed to start feeling better." Kate worked loose enough that she could pivot and fold in close to Casey.

"I think I've already made her acquaintance. And to tell the truth, I don't know how you could possibly feel any better; you feel marvelous to me." They stood in the kitchen and swayed to the soundless music playing in their hearts.

"Would you do me the honor of coming to my bed, Ms. Bingham?"

"I was hoping you'd ask, Ms. Marsden."

They left the kitchen and crossed the great room, turning off lights as they went. Once inside the bedroom, they carefully—almost reverently—helped one another undress.

Then they spent the rest of the night making the promises of their fortunes come true.

Chapter 11

"You really look terrific, Kate." Casey kissed her twice to prove the point. "You're sure you're willing to brave Thanksgiving with my family?" They were standing just inside the door to Casey's house.

Kate pulled free from Casey and leaned down to rub Roger as he did his canine dance of welcome around her feet. Kate had spent virtually every minute of each of the past four weekends at Casey's house; Roger had come to regard Kate as a regular part of the family. For her part, Kate, who had never owned an indoor pet, was beginning to think of herself as lacking proper accessories if she didn't have several dog and cat hairs adorning her clothing whenever she went out.

"What's to brave?" Kate replied as she stood. "We'll help put the meal on the table at your mother's, make conversation with your sisters and brother and assorted other kith and kin, eat way too much, bag some leftovers, and head back here." She grinned knowingly as she dropped a hand on Casey's shoulder. "You do know that I'm not planning on having any pumpkin pie—you're the only dessert I want, Thanksgiving or any other day."

She enfolded Casey in a snug embrace and nuzzled her neck. "Maybe we should just skip all the appetizers and main course trappings and go right for the good stuff."

"Tempting though that sounds, dear heart, I think we'd better go to Mother's. Daddy has been really out of it this week with Christine and her family staying there. I wish they'd have gone to a motel like I asked them to." Casey drew her hands down Kate's arms and let her lips linger on Kate's fingertips as she relinquished her grip around her. "You'd think with the kind of money she's making selling houses these days she could spring for a room and help save what's left of Daddy's ability to cope."

"Maybe she just wanted to stay at the house so she could help your mother get ready for today."

"You've never met Christine, have you?" Casey turned and headed toward the kitchen. Kate followed. "The day Christine lifts a finger to help Mother—or anyone else—will be the day the sun rises at midnight."

"Not exactly the Martha Stewart of North Florida, huh?" Kate asked as they cleared the doorway.

"If there's some payoff in it for her, then Christine is at the head of the line, but when it comes to pitching in just for the heck of it, forget it."

"You're sure everybody is all right with my tagging along? I mean, this is really a gathering for your family . . ."

"Two things, Kate Bingham." Casey looked Kate squarely in the eye. "First, as far as I'm concerned *you* are part of my family—the most important part, in fact. Second, I've been on the phone with both of my sisters during the week and they're both really glad that you're coming. They didn't seem surprised in the least when I told them that you'd be with us for Thanksgiving, so I'm guessing that Mother must have at least mentioned you to them over the past month."

Casey gestured toward an array of homemade pies on the kitchen table. "I'm sorry to hear you say you won't be partaking of dessert, Kate. There are women all over western Carolina who'd kill to have a slice of one of these heavenly concoctions."

"Why, Kayrun Clarice! I declare! I had no idea you were a whiz with a whisk."

"I'll have you know I am a woman of many talents. Just because you've only witnessed my prowess in the bedroom speaks more about you than it does about me."

"Seriously, sweetie, these look great. What all did you make?"

One by one, Casey paraded her creations: "Mince, cherry, strawberry rhubarb, peach, and, of course, pumpkin," she finished and made a half-bow from the waist. "And I made a cranberry salad and some whole wheat rolls, too." She proceeded to open the refrigerator and pull out the tray of individual congealed salads and then opened a drawer and extracted three dozen rolls wrapped in plastic bags. "I think we'd better use your car to haul all this to Mother's. There wouldn't be room in the cab of the moo mobile."

"Sure, that's fine, Case." She surveyed all the eats Casey had prepared. "You have really been working your fingers to the bone, haven't you?"

"From the minute you pulled out of here Monday morning to head back to Atlanta. I did the bread and two pies on Monday, the rest of the pies on Tuesday, and the salad yesterday. Believe it or not, the salad was probably the hardest. I had to hand chop all the cranberries and pecans, and then I had to grease all the little molds with mayonnaise so that the darn things would come out once the gelatin set. And of course, I only have six molds, and since there will be fourteen of us at dinner, I had to make the whole recipe three times." Casey swooned for dramatic effect. "A woman's work is never done."

"Well, I can see we'll have to reconsider how we spend our weekends. I thought your greatest skill in the food department was memorizing the phone numbers of all the carryout places in Delano. I see now that I was misinformed."

"Hey, I was only trying to make the most of what little time we have together. If you'd rather have me whipping up gourmet repasts than finding new ways to make your toes curl under, then so it shall be." The two stood face to face in the center of the room, smiling warmly at one another.

"I know that look, Kate Bingham. Come on, let's get these cattle to Texas." Casey slapped her imaginary riding crop at her imaginary horse.

"Only if you promise me that before this day is done I can sleep naked with you in the bunkhouse."

"Deal," Casey agreed with an outstretched hand.

It took four trips to get everything out of the house and properly lined up on the backseat of Kate's Volvo. Casey went back inside, and Kate double-checked to be sure things were wedged in place. She went to the door and whistled for the dog. Roger got one last lap of freedom around the yard while Kate watched from the stoop.

Casey came to the doorway and cracked the door. "Need anything else inside before we head out?"

"Nope, ready when you are," Kate replied. "Come on, Roger," she called. "Back in the house, buster," she directed as he scooted past her and Casey.

Casey turned the key in the deadbolt. The two women clasped hands as they walked the dozen or so paces to the car.

"No matter what else the day might bring, I'm thankful to be spending it with you." Casey squeezed Kate's hand as she spoke.

"No matter what else, me too," Kate concurred.

Chapter 12

"Dammit! Will all of you just get out of my house! I don't know who you are, and I don't want you here!" Burr threw the basket of rolls in the general direction of the far end of the table.

"Daddy!"

"Burr!"

"Grandpa!"

The Marsden family assembled around the Thanksgiving feast reacted in unison.

"I mean it. Get out of here, all of you. You have no right to come into my house and eat my food." Burr looked around at the strangers who bedeviled him, then abruptly rose from his chair and lurched toward the rear of the house.

Nora and her children looked beseechingly at one another. "I'll go," Casey said simply. Kate caught her eye; Casey shook her head as if to say "no," then she left the table and set off after her father.

"Should we keep eating, Grandma?" Kevin, the youngest of the four grandchildren asked, giving voice to the same question that was on everyone's mind.

"Yes, love. Eat what's on your plate. Granddaddy is just not feeling very good today. He didn't mean what he said." Nora was visibly shaken by Burr's outburst. Her expression and her tone belied the sincerity of her words. "Aunt Casey made lots of pies for all of us to have for dessert. I bet Granddaddy will want to have some pie with us after a while." She picked up her fork and went through the motions of eating what remained of her meal.

"Mother, don't you think it's time Daddy saw a specialist someplace?" Christine asked after a few minutes of strained silence.

"Not now, Christine." Nora nodded toward the youngsters grouped near her at the table. "Little pitchers . . ." For several minutes, the only sound was the clink of utensils against china.

"The turkey is really tender, Nora," offered Darren's wife, Judy. "Mine always turns out like shoe leather."

"Yeah, Mom, the turkey and everything is just great," Margie seconded. "Thanks for all the trouble you went to."

"Oh, it was nothing, baby. I'm just glad to have everyone home." Nora smiled weakly at her youngest child. "Well, almost everyone. It would have been nice if BJ could have been here, too, but he said he couldn't come all the way from California for both Thanksgiving and Christmas, so I guess we'll just have to wait till next month to see him."

There was a palpable air of relief as the conversation shifted to safe topics. The remainder of the meal was passed with Nora and her children and in-laws (with occasional comments from Kate) talking about air fares, holiday plans, the weather, and the grandchildren's school vacations—anything but the man who had stormed from the table, calling them aliens and thieves.

The last declination of another serving of anything had just been issued when Casey re-emerged from her parents' bedroom.

"He's sleeping," she said in reply to the unasked question. "I turned on NPR. The music really seemed to help." She resumed her seat next to Kate. "Just too much noise and confusion for him, I think."

"Well, let's get these leftovers put away before the germs have a chance to find them," Nora suggested as though Casey had never spoken. "I know I'm going to want to try at least two kinds of pie."

"Mother—" Casey began; her mother cut her off before she could form another word.

"Don't fuss at me. I know you helped get the meal ready to put on the table, so it's your sisters' turn to clean up." Nora stood and grabbed two bowls of vegetables. "Christine, Margie, let's go. Judy, you won't mind helping, will you? I know you men just want to get downstairs to that blasted football game on TV. Kids, you go on to the basement and get out from underfoot." The four grandchildren seized their reprieve and dashed down the stairwell.

Nora vanished into the kitchen. All eyes turned to Casey. "I've tried to tell you guys that this is what's been going on for months," she said, barely above a whisper. "He is completely locked up in some secret world inside his head, and she's in contention for best supporting actress. Now maybe you'll start to believe me when I tell you that there's big trouble in this house."

Nora came back around the corner into the dining room. "Girls, get with it. I want to see this table cleared and the dishwasher loaded in ten minutes. Kate and Casey, go downstairs and make sure the little ones aren't playing with Daddy's model cars. He'd have a fit if they were messing with his collection." She gathered up the relish tray and the bowl of mashed potatoes. "Guys, you just sit tight. Coffee and pie will be on the way as soon as we get the meal put up."

The next couple of hours were calm and quiet. Max and Ed, Nora's sons-in-law, sat in the basement with Darren watching the Cowboys beat up on Detroit on the football field. Cousins Kevin and Andy busied themselves in the storeroom off the basement rec room making forts out of cardboard boxes while the girl cousins, Susan and Angela, pestered their fathers and uncles for pony rides on crossed knees. Eventually, they pulled out coloring books and crayons and retreated to a corner of the rec room.

Upstairs, Nora and her daughters and Kate and Judy sat around the table drinking endless cups of coffee making small talk. If anyone mentioned Burr, his illness, or his earlier outburst, Nora immediately steered the conversation in some other direction. It was late afternoon when Burr ambled out from the bedroom.

"Well, there sit all my pretty ones," he observed as he came into the dining room. "Nora, is it just my imagination or did I miss lunch today?"

It was like a bad grade-school enactment of Rip Van Winkle's awakening. Burr was no longer agitated and upset, but he likewise wasn't able to call his daughters by name nor apparently was he able to remember anything that had transpired before Casey had used classical music on National Public Radio to lull him to sleep.

"Who's downstairs? I hear the TV."

"Darren and Max and Ed, Daddy," Margie supplied. "And the kids are down there, too."

"What kids? The neighbor kids?" Burr seemed genuinely perplexed.

"Our kids, honey," Nora replied. "Our grandbabies."

"Huh," Burr grunted, not quite a question, not quite an acknowledgment. "I'm hungry."

"I'll fix you a plate," Nora offered as she rose from her chair. "Do you want turkey and all the trimmings?"

"Turkey? A fellow would think it was Thanksgiving or something. Sure, I'll have some turkey." Burr followed Nora into the kitchen.

Nora returned to the dining room a few minutes later. "I think we should just let him eat alone out there. He must have slept so hard that he can't remember what day it is." She gave a nervous laugh. "I think I'll fix up some snack trays for later so that everybody can just help themselves to an evening meal." She withdrew to the kitchen again.

"There, that should satisfy everybody," Nora observed, wiping her hands on a dishtowel as she re-entered the dining room. "Casey, help me bring things in here so that we can load up plates from the buffet."

Casey and Nora made several trips bearing serving platters of leftovers and sandwich makings. There were bowls of chips and dips, plates of cookies and sweets, and a tray of crab salad and crackers.

"Mom, we just ate a few hours ago," Margie protested. "There's no need for all this."

"Well, at least it's here if anyone wants it," Nora rejoined. "Kate, will you run downstairs and tell the men and the little ones that they're welcome to come help themselves?"

One by one, the men wandered by the buffet and loaded plates, then descended back to the basement for the rest of the football game. The women helped the children fix sandwiches and select cookies and shooed them off to sit with Max, Ed, and Darren.

"I'm still too full," Kate declared. "Would anyone like to play some cards or a board game?"

"Sure," Judy agreed. "That would be fun. What do you suggest?"

"I've got a couple of things out in the trunk of my car. I'll go get them." Kate dashed out into the early twilight, grateful for the brace of cool air against her face. Once back inside, she held up the options. "There's the old standby, Scrabble, or I've got Clue, or there's Pictionary."

"Not Scrabble or Clue," Christine whined. "You have to think too hard. What's Pictionary?"

"You divide up into teams and draw pictures of words on cards that you pick from the pile," Kate explained. "Your teammates have to figure out what it is that you're drawing. Sort of like charades done with pencil and paper. It's lots of fun."

"I'm willing to give it a try," Margie ventured.

"Me too," Judy concurred.

"Mother, you'll play won't you?" Casey encouraged.

"Oh, I don't know—I'm not very good at games."

"You have to, Nora, or the teams won't be even," Kate stated. "Let's you, Judy, and I take on those daughters of yours."

As they were setting up the game board on the dining room table, Burr drifted in, stains from his late dinner obvious on his shirt and a roll still in his hand.

"Sweetie, the girls and I are going to play a game. Do you want to take my place or at least sit down and watch us?" Nora invited.

"No, I'm just going to sit over here," Burr replied. He dragged a chair from the dining suite over beside the buffet. "I think I'm still hungry." He helped himself to some crab salad and then had a couple of cookies.

Soon the two teams were having a rowdy time trying to come up with ways to draw vice, erode, government, orbit, bad breath, snowstorm, tutu, or whatever else cropped up on the category cards from the game. Periodically, one of the women would look over to see how Burr was doing. He was making up for his earlier lost opportunity at a Thanksgiving banquet and busily snacking his way through the many treats that Nora had laid out on the sideboard.

"Where's Daddy?" Casey made no attempt to camouflage her concern.

Suddenly, it seemed, Burr had disappeared.

"He was at the buffet eating, the last time I looked." Christine's voice sounded pinched and tinny. "He must have gone downstairs."

"I'll look." Casey bolted for the basement and was back in a heartbeat. "He's not down there. The guys swear they haven't seen him."

"Burr?" Nora called. "Burr? Where are you?" Hysteria edged into her voice.

"He can't have gone far. He was here just a few minutes ago," Margie reasoned.

"What's up?" Darren asked as he cleared the last stair.

"We don't know where Daddy is," Christine replied. "He was over in the corner by the buffet, but now he's gone."

"Did he go outside?" Darren pressed.

"I don't know. I don't think so." Nora started to wring her hands. "We've got to find him."

"All the cars are still here," Darren noted as he looked out the dining room window, "so he can't have gotten very far. I'll get Max and Ed and we'll check around out in the yard."

"You're sure he's not in the storeroom or his workshop in the basement or out in the garage?" Margie demanded.

"Well, he could have slipped past us, I guess. We really weren't paying much attention to anything but the game on TV. We maybe even dozed off a time or two."

"OK, Darren, get the guys and go check the yard," Casey directed. "Christine, you and Margie go downstairs and look everywhere. With all the stuff stacked in the storeroom, you need to be sure to look really carefully. Mother, you and Judy need to round up the kids and see if they saw him. They need to understand that this isn't just some grown-up version of hide and seek."

"I'll make my way through the rooms at the back of the house," Kate proposed.

"Thanks. I'm going to call a couple of the near-by neighbors just in case he's wandered over to someone's house." Casey headed for the phone on the kitchen wall while everyone else scattered to their assigned places.

When Nora and Burr built their retirement house, they expected that their five children, the in-laws, and the grandchildren would be frequent visitors, so in addition to the master bedroom suite, they had included three other good-sized rooms, two of which had adjoining baths, so that there'd be plenty of room for the extended family. One of the rooms was set up as a permanent guestroom. All of Burr's engineering reference books and historical project files were housed in the second of the spare rooms. Nora used the third one as her sewing room and the place where she and the grandkids would gather to do puzzles, read books, or finger paint.

Kate went to the master bedroom first. She checked the shower stall and the bathtub, both walk-in closets, and under the bed. There was no sign of Burr. She went to Burr's study next. The file cabinets, bookcases, oversized desk, and day bed left few places where Burr could be. She looked in the closet, under the desk, in the bathroom, but again, came up empty. Nora's sewing room was the same story.

That left only the guest bedroom. Since Christine and Max were staying in that room, she didn't think that Burr would venture in, given how distressed he was by any disruption in his routine. She put her hand on the knob and was surprised to find the door locked. She thought of calling for Casey or some of the others, but decided against it. She stepped back across the hall to Burr's study and retrieved the letter opener from the pen holder on his desk. It was just thin enough to slip into the hole in the center of the knob. She gave a twist and heard the lock pop free.

Nothing in her wildest imaginings could have prepared her for the scene that greeted her when she pushed the door back.

Chapter 13

Burr Marsden lay facedown across the queen-sized bed that was against the far wall of the room.

"Oh my God; he's dead." Just as the thought made its way across Kate's mind, Burr stirred slightly and retched, spewing what little remained in his stomach onto the floor in front of him. Many of Kate's senses were engaged at once. The sights, smells, and sounds that assaulted her as she took a half-step into the room sent her reeling. It was evident that Burr had been violently sick for some period of time. As she swept a glance around the room, it appeared that no surface had been spared. Open dresser drawers, Christine and Max's open luggage, the little tote bags and backpacks that their daughter, Angela's, things were in, shoes lined up at the foot of the bed, trash cans, the upholstered chair, the lamp shades, the nightstands, the bedspread, the scatter rugs—everything bore the signs of Burr's intestinal distress.

The stench hit her like a slap across the face, and it was all she could do to fight down her own gag reflex. "Stay calm, Kate," she admonished herself. "You can handle this."

Just then, Kate heard Casey, Nora, Judy, and the two little girls approaching down the hallway.

"Don't come in here," Kate commanded as she turned back toward them. "I've found him."

"Is he all right? What happened? Where is he? What's that smell? Should I call a doctor?" The questions tumbled out one on top of another. Even though Kate's body was partially blocking the doorway, it wasn't enough to prevent the newcomers from seeing the catastrophe, and even if she could have shielded their eyes, there was nothing she could do about the reeking odor roiling in every corner of the room.

Nora tried to push past Kate, but Kate caught her by the shoulders and pushed her back.

"Oh, no!" The words barely passed Nora's lips as she slumped to the floor.

"Mother! Nora!" Casey and Judy cried in unison.

Susan and Angela began to cry. "Granddaddy's sick and Grandmommy just died," Angela wailed.

"For God's sake, Christine! Darren! Max! Somebody get down here and help us," Casey called. "Oh, jeez, I think I'm going to be sick."

Kate stepped up directly in front of Casey's face. "No, you are not. Take a couple of really deep breaths and think about—about— anything else. Think about your dog and cats. Go get the men to come carry your mom into her bedroom. She's fainted and she needs your help. Now, go!"

"But my dad—the mess—the rug—"

"Never mind about that, Casey. I'll deal with this. Judy, once you've gotten the girls settled, bring me a box of trash bags, a bucket, some Lysol, and every roll of paper towels in the house and leave them outside the door here."

Casey took off at a dead run down the hallway and out the front door, calling for her brother and brothers-in-law. Judy took Susan and Angela back downstairs, where she found Margie and Christine still combing the storeroom off the garage and provided them with a recap of the horrors she had glimpsed in the guest bedroom. While Margie and Christine raced to their mother's side, Judy explained to Kevin and Andy that they would have to entertain the little girls while the adults took care of some problems upstairs. Then she set about gathering the supplies that Kate had asked for.

Meanwhile, Kate was threading her way around and among the puddles and stains that littered the guest bedroom floor. Blessedly, Burr seemed to have finally purged himself of every one of the many, many edibles he had consumed, unsupervised, while sitting at the sideboard.

"Come on, Burr. Let's get you cleaned up." She helped him roll over and swung his feet onto the floor. Not surprisingly, the front of his shirt and pants were a wretched, stinking jumble. "He's just a baby who spit up his bottle," she coaxed herself, silently. "He needs your help, Kate. Think about elephants. Think about waterfalls. Think about tutus, orbits, snowstorms . . ." She forced herself to bring back to mind as many of the Pictionary cards as she could. "Was it really just ten minutes ago I was sitting with Casey's family playing a game?" she wondered, incredulous.

She half-dragged, half-carried Burr to the bathroom. She gingerly undid the buttons on his shirt and loosened his belt. She carefully pulled his clothes off him and folded them in on themselves so that the worst of his mess was contained within.

"Can you get into the shower, Burr?" she urged. "Just let the water wash over you for a little while."

To her relief, Burr seemed perfectly willing to let Kate—someone he often greeted as though she were a total stranger whenever Casey brought her to the house—treat him as though they were family. He was subdued and cooperative. After he had spent a few minutes in the shower, she turned off the shower head and helped him wrap a towel around himself. "Dry yourself off, Burr. I'm going to get you some clothes."

Kate went out into the bedroom and opened the closet door. To her dismay, Burr had managed to make a couple of deposits on that floor as well, but the clothes hanging on the bar and on the hooks on the back of the door seemed to have escaped the trajectories. She grabbed what she assumed to be a pair of Max's pajamas and returned to the bathroom.

"Here, Burr. Put these on." Burr was standing buck naked in the middle of the bathroom floor, shivering. The wet towel lay in a heap around his feet.

Legs in leg holes and arms in arm holes was too complex a concept for him to handle alone, so Kate had to help him get into the pajamas.

"I'm hungry," Burr allowed.

"We'll eat breakfast in a little while," Kate assured him, "but now, it's time for bed."

Ever so carefully she led Burr from the bathroom, through the bedroom, out the door and down the hall to the master bedroom, pulling the door to the guest room closed behind her as they left. Nora had been revived and was lying back, ashen, propped up on pillows leaning against the headboard. She had shooed everyone except Casey from the room.

"Hi, honey. I'm hungry," Burr announced as he cleared the doorway.

Nora stared stone-faced at her husband.

"First bed, then breakfast, Burr," Kate said gently as she brought him around to his side of the bed. "Get under the covers." She held the comforter and sheet up so that he could lie down.

"I think he's exhausted." Kate looked at Nora as she spoke. "Probably the best thing for both of you would be to just call it a day and try to get some rest."

Nora made no reply, but stared glassy-eyed into the far corner of the room.

"Come on, Case." Kate took Casey by the elbow. Her color wasn't much better than her mother's. "I think you need some fresh air."

Kate and Casey walked back down the hall to the living room where the rest of the family was gathered. "Would a couple of you take Casey outside for a while, please? I think it would do her good to be outdoors for a little bit."

"Sure," Darren offered. "Hell of a Thanksgiving, huh, little sister?" He wrapped an arm protectively around Casey. "Want to come along, love?" he asked his wife.

"No, I'm going downstairs to check on the kids. You two go on," Judy replied.

Darren grabbed his jacket and one of his mother's sweaters for Casey from the front hall closet and let them both out the door.

"I'm going back to deal with—" Kate canted her head toward the rear of the house. She couldn't find an appropriate word to describe what awaited her in the guest bedroom.

She paused just for a moment to wait for the offer of help that she knew would not be forthcoming. She turned and began a slow walk down the hallway. "Bad breath, vice, erode." Kate started the mental litany of all of the words from the Pictionary cards that she could remember. "Corduroy, crumb, elope, oxygen," she continued silently. "Smelling salts, glob, pail."

With a sigh, she reopened the door to the guest bedroom and with it, the door to her memories of Ray Bingham.

Chapter 14

It was nearly midnight when Casey and Kate pulled up at Casey's house.

"I'll supervise Roger's liberation and clean out the litter boxes while you put the food away, OK?" Kate offered as she and Casey stepped out of the car.

"Sure," Casey replied. "Can you help me get these bags of left-overs into the house?"

The two women gathered the assortment from the backseat of Kate's Volvo and walked across the damp grass to the front door of the house. Casey shifted her armload and eased the key into the lock. The door had barely moved on its hinges before Roger wedged his face in the crack and bolted between them.

"Poor guy. He's had a long day," Casey observed as the dog dashed past them. "I hope he didn't make any messes in the house. I've had all the messes I can stand for one day."

"Yeah, I'd second that sentiment," Kate concurred.

Casey flipped on a couple of lights as she headed for the kitchen. Kate followed with her load of containers with the remains of the Marsdens' Thanksgiving meal.

"OK, next stop, kitty boxes," Kate said as she deposited her collection of tubs, baggies, and foil packages onto the countertop. "Then I'll make sure Roger hasn't ruptured his bladder out in the yard."

She stepped into the utility room just off the kitchen and scooped the two litter pans that stood by the washer and dryer. She tied a knot in the neck of the plastic grocery bag and opened the door to the back yard, turning on the exterior light as she stepped into the frosty night air. Roger heard her lift the lid of the trashcan as she deposited the bag into it; he raced around the corner of the house and dropped to his haunches at Kate's feet.

"Hey, pal," Kate cooed as she knelt down to pet him. "I missed you today." Roger licked her face to show his agreement. "Come on, let's go stretch your legs a little more." Woman and dog trotted along the side of the house back to the front yard. The halogen yard light cast its yellow-pink light from high atop its pole. It backlit the naked tree branches making eerie jagged bolts—almost like netherworld lightning—across the inky sky.

Kate and Roger romped and played beneath the two moons—one real and one courtesy of the local electrical membership cooperative—of the late November sky, both of them grateful for the freedom from the oppressions of earlier in the day and oblivious to the passing of time. Kate glanced at her wristwatch.

"Omigosh, Roger, it's nearly one o'clock in the morning," she called softly. "We've been out here for an hour. Come on, we need to get inside." She slapped her thigh and the dog scampered to her side.

She checked the front door first. As she suspected, Casey had turned the thumb latch as they went in. Locked tight. They traced their way to the back door and entered the utility room. Most of the lights in the house had been turned off, but there was enough illumination for Kate to find her way through the kitchen and great room, down the hallway, and into the bedroom. Casey was lying in bed, her back to the doorway. Roger took his cue from Kate and was extra quiet as they entered the room. Kate pointed to the dog bed in the corner by the chest of drawers and Roger dutifully went over and climbed in. The two cats were, as usual, curled snugly around one another at the foot of the bed, just below Casey's feet.

A small night light in the bathroom let Kate see well enough to take off her makeup and pierced earrings and to give her teeth a quick brushing. She shed her clothes and shook into one of Casey's long-sleeved T-shirts that she had preempted as sleepwear.

Once back in the bedroom, Kate could see that Casey had rolled over so that her back was now toward the middle of the queen-sized bed. Light as a feather, Kate lay down on the bed and glided under the sheet and down coverlet.

"I was afraid you'd gone back to Atlanta." Casey's voice was strained and small.

"Oh, sweetie. I'm sorry I woke you." Kate edged closer to Casey's back and draped her arm across her midsection. "Roger and I just lost track of time. It's a pretty night, even if it's a little cold." She kissed the back of Casey's neck. "Why would you think I'd gone back to Atlanta?"

"After that holy hell at Mother's today, if I had the choice, I'd run as far and as fast as I could." Casey paused briefly and then continued. "And I wasn't sleeping. I've been lying here trying to figure out what I can say to you to apologize and to thank you and to beg you—" Her voice cracked and she started to cry.

Kate pulled Casey tightly to her. "Stop, babe. Please don't cry." She lifted herself up on one elbow so that her face was right next to Casey's ear. "You don't owe me an apology or thanks or anything else. And what could you possibly need to beg me for? Don't you know by now that I'd give you anything that's mine to give?"

Casey shuddered and sobbed. "Oh, Kate! You're just saying that. There's no way in the world that you're going to stick around after what you had to deal with today. I'm not even sure I can stick around, but they're my parents. I have . . ."

Kate pulled back from Casey so that she could sit up and reached over to turn on the lamp on the nightstand. She took Casey by the shoulder. "Roll over, love. Let me see your beautiful face." Casey did as Kate asked and sat up, her back against the bookcase headboard. The soft glow from the bulb showed Casey's swollen eyes and tear-streaked cheeks.

"How long have you been crying?"

"Since you went outside after cleaning the litter boxes. I kept waiting to hear your car start, but then I decided I didn't want to know when you left, so I just came back here and crawled into bed."

The cats, roused from their slumber, decided it was a good time to get some attention. Caboodle stood, arched her back, and edged onto Casey's lap. Kit followed her lead and was soon elongated beside Kate's outstretched legs. Both women began mindlessly stroking their furry companions.

Kate waited a moment before speaking. "So just why is it you think I'd pull out of here in the middle of the night without so much as a good-bye?"

"What possible reason could you have for staying?"

"Well, for starters, how about the fact that I've fallen in love with you?"

"But Kate, you didn't sign on for anything so awful as what went on at my parents' house today. Nobody should ever have to put up with something like that."

"So there were some lumps in the mashed potatoes your mother made," Kate joked lightly. "Big deal."

Casey wasn't in the mood for humor. "Kate, don't try to dodge this. I just can't imagine how you did what you did. I mean cleaning up the second bedroom and getting Daddy showered and into bed and . . ." She paused, not sure how to continue.

"I simply did what needed to be done. I'm pretty good at shutting down my mind and going someplace else in my imagination if I have to."

"I still don't know how you did it, Kate. I get sick to my stomach just thinking about it."

"So don't think about it, Casey. It's over and done. We're home and together and in another couple of hours, we'll have a brand new morning to greet."

"But Kate—"

Kate cut her off before she could say anything more.

"Remember that I told you my dad had a condition something like what your dad seems to be suffering from?"

"Sure," Casey nodded.

"I've never told you any of the details, though." Kate cleared her throat, turned to look at Casey beside her, then let her eyes fall out of focus as she gazed back in time more than half a dozen years.

"My dad's illness—it had some ridiculous multiword name that I never could remember—basically reduced him to the mental capacity of a two-year-old. Oh, he still had words in his vocabulary, but like as not, he'd call a chair a plow or a plate a pillow and whatever he said came out all jumbled and tangled like pages torn from nine different books. If he went to wash his hands, unless someone was there to remind him to turn off the water and dry his hands, he'd stand at the sink for an hour or more rubbing his hands under the faucet. And sometimes, he *would* turn off the water, and then still stand there washing his hands in an imaginary stream of water."

"Sounds a lot like my dad, Kate."

"He lived alone on our farm for all those years after my mom died. I got back to Wisconsin to see him a couple of times a year, and eventually, I realized that he was having some problems with remembering things, but I thought that was just what happened as people got older. I was pretty wrapped up in my work and I always hated being away from Nikki for more than a day or two, so my trips got shorter and farther between. I didn't have a clue about just how bad things were getting. I figured that since my sisters were still only an hour away from him, they were keeping tabs on his welfare. I should have known better."

"I bet your sisters were doing what mine have been doing for the past year or more—ignoring something that was just too painful to look at."

"Maybe. I hadn't thought of it that way. It seemed to me that they were just neglecting him, but they might have just been protecting themselves." She took a deep breath. "And I knew I should have been spending more time with him. I'm sure my guilty conscience made me all the more eager to blame my sisters for something that was just as much my fault as theirs."

"So your dad forgot words and washed his hands a lot. That doesn't sound so bad."

"If that were as far as it went, it wouldn't have been. It got a lot worse." Kate shifted herself and repositioned the pillows behind her back. "I'm not sure I should tell you some of this stuff."

Casey inched closer to Kate, Caboodle still in her lap. "No, I want you to tell me. This is all uncharted territory for me. Knowing what you went through will help me deal with Daddy."

"OK, but if it gets to be too much, tell me to stop." Kate curled her lower lip and blew out a puff of air. "It was about two years before he died. I hadn't been back to see him for several months. My sisters were busy with their jobs and kids and houses, so they hadn't been going to see him, either. He was still driving—even though in hindsight I know that he shouldn't have been—and had managed to get to Madison to visit my sisters a time or two, so no one had been back to the old home place in Janesville in quite a while.

"It was Thanksgiving—oh, gosh, till this very minute I had forgotten that—anyway, it was Thanksgiving and I had just completed arrangements with DeWitt and company to move from Detroit to New Haven after the first of the year. I decided to take advantage of still being fairly close to Wisconsin and made the trip to Janesville to spend the holiday with my dad.

"Some time since the last time anyone had been to his house, he had forgotten the concept of indoor plumbing. Any time he needed to urinate or defecate, he apparently just did—on the floors, on the furniture, on the stairway, in wastebaskets—everywhere. It defies description." Kate shuddered as she recalled the discovery.

Casey reached over and took Kate's hand. "So what did you do?"

"First I called my sisters and told them to get their sorry selves down to Janesville. They pitched a fit because it was Thanksgiving and it would ruin all their plans and preparations. I told them 'Too damn bad. Dad needs you here right now.' Then I tried to talk to my dad about what he had done. Of course the stench in the house was too much to endure, so I took him outside to his truck, thinking we could sit out there and talk and run the engine to stay warm if we had to. Imagine my delight to find that he'd crapped and peed in both the cab and the load bed of his truck. We ended up sitting in my rental car while we waited for Martha and Jolene."

"Martha and Jolene? Your sisters? Kate, do you know that this is the first time you've ever mentioned your sisters' names?" Casey interrupted. "I'm sorry; I was just surprised to hear you call them by name. Go on with what you were telling me."

"Do you know that he actually tried to convince me the dog had caused the pandemonium that was everywhere? When I reminded him that he hadn't had a dog on the property in almost five years and that even when he did, the dog was never allowed in the house, then he said that the hired hand had done it and that he'd had to fire him for what he'd done."

"Did he actually have a hired hand?"

"No, of course not. He hadn't done any farming in years. He was renting the land out to one of the neighbors' sons. He still lived in the old farmhouse where he'd lived since he got married. Nothing he said had any basis in reality. Talking to him was like talking to a complete stranger. To tell the truth, I wasn't altogether sure that he knew who I was that day. On some level, he seemed to know that I was familiar and safe, but he treated me like I was some interloper who had showed up at his house questioning him about everything he'd done and accusing him of things he couldn't possibly be responsible for. It was all so sad.

"It was obvious to me that somewhere inside his head he knew that everything was terribly wrong, but just what or why or when or how was completely beyond what he could comprehend."

"So did your sisters come and help you figure out what to do?"

"By the time they got themselves organized and dealt with whatever they had to do about putting their Thanksgiving dinner on hold, it took them almost three hours to get there. By then, I'd about used up all the gas in my rental car letting the engine idle so that Dad and I didn't freeze our toes. When they finally did get there, I told them what I'd found inside the house. At first, they wouldn't believe me. They insisted on going in to see for themselves. Of course, Jolene almost fainted and Martha threw up, so then I had three problems instead of just one."

"Hearing all this, I'm even more amazed that you were able to do what you did at Mother's today."

"Huh. I guess that scene at Dad's that day was my dress rehearsal. I gotta tell you, though, I sure hope this was the last performance I have to participate in."

"So is that when you put your dad in a nursing home?"

"We couldn't—well, at least not that very day. It was Thanksgiving, remember. The administrative offices at all three of the homes in Janesville were closed. Once I got Martha and Jolene sort of back on their feet, I left Dad with them in their car at the farmhouse while I went to find a pay phone and get some gas. All I got was recordings on their answering machines telling me that they were closed till the following Monday."

"I guess one of your sisters must have taken your dad home with them for the weekend, then . . ."

"A reasonable assumption, but way off the mark, my dear," Kate snorted. "They made every excuse under the sun for why they couldn't do it. When I look back on it now, I should have just left them out of it and taken care of things myself. I ended up renting a room for him and me in a fleabag motel on the edge of town. Most of the decent places were booked with folks traveling for the holiday.

Besides, I didn't want to risk having him in a nice place—who knew what he might do?"

"Did it go all right?"

"Not really. I got a room with two beds so I could sort of keep an eye on him. That first night, I woke up to hear him using the metal trashcan in the room as a urinal. When I tried to remind him that he was supposed to use the bathroom for that, he told me that when you're a soldier out in the woods, it's OK to just go behind a tree. I think that's when I really realized just how far gone his mind was."

"Oh, Kate, I'm so sorry." Casey hesitated before continuing. "Do you think the same thing will happen to my dad?"

"It's impossible to say, sweetie. Once he was institutionalized, I did a lot of research into dementia to see if there was something more that could be done for my dad. About the only thing the literature could tell me was that each case is different and that there's no way to predict what will happen to anybody or on what timetable it might occur." She scratched an itch above her eyebrow. "One thing, though, that seems real common is that someone can cruise along for months or even years in a slow—almost imperceptible—decline, but then all of a sudden, they just plummet to a much lower level." Kate used her free hand to draw two horizontal lines in the air to demonstrate her point.

The cats, convinced that all the conversation must be an indication that it was morning and time for canned cat food in the kitchen, stirred and commenced their "C'mon, let's eat" dance.

"No, guys, it's still the middle of the night," Casey commented, trying to calm Caboodle.

"Well, actually, they have a point," Kate corrected. "It *is* the middle of the night, but you and I haven't had anything to eat since early afternoon. What with all that transpired later in the day, we never got so much as a bite beyond what we had for dinner way back at about one in the afternoon. That was almost 14 hours ago."

"Now that you mention it, I am a little hungry; I was sure I'd never have an appetite again," Casey rejoined.

"The miracle of the human animal. Just when we think we've got ourselves figured out, we fool ourselves." Kate stretched and yawned. "I'm getting stiff from sitting like this. A walk to the kitchen and a little snack might be just the ticket."

"I think you're right." Casey followed suit and extended her arms high above her head. "What do you want to eat?"

"Good grief, Casey. It's the day after Thanksgiving. What else? A turkey sandwich."

Chapter 15

Casey and Kate heaped slices of leftover white meat from the bird that Nora Marsden had roasted onto slices of toasted bread. Roger was the beneficiary of a number of morsels that happened to find their way to his lips. The cats made faces and uttered their version of "yuck" when Kate put little bites down for them.

"What the heck? It's only three hours till they'd get fed anyhow. I might as well open a can for them now and save us the pain of their whining," Casey sighed.

After all the residents of the household had satisfied their stomachs, the five of them (two weary women, one dog, and two cats) sat quietly in the kitchen for quite some time.

"Let's go back to bed, Kate."

"You know, I think we might feel worse for getting a couple of hours of sleep than if we just stay up and forge on through the day. We told your mom and Christine that we'd be over there early to help with whatever else needs doing and to see just how much damage your dad did yesterday."

"Let's at least go somewhere more comfortable than these hard chairs," Casey suggested.

They went into the great room. Casey rolled the in-line switch on the cord of the hanging lamp in the corner near the entertainment unit. "Some music?"

"Sure."

Casey slipped three New Age CDs into the player and turned the volume down so that the soft pianos and flutes were barely audible.

Kate was sitting on the sofa, her legs pulled up beside her. Casey dropped down on the other end of the sofa. "Should I turn up the heat?"

"No, I'll just use this throw—unless you want to run the furnace." She lifted the soft, loosely knit rose and teal blanket from the back of the sofa and arranged it over herself.

"Huh-uh. I'm fine for now." Just as Casey was about to swing her legs out in front of her down the sofa between her and Kate, first one and then the second cat jumped into the open space. Roger ambled over, sprang up from the floor, and flopped down beside the cats.

"Looks like something has come between us, dear," Kate teased.

"Are you sure that it isn't something more serious than two felines with salmon breath and a dog that's had too much turkey?" Casey measured her words as she continued. "I guess I still can't believe that you're not going to vanish."

Kate held Casey's gaze in her own and then spoke slowly and carefully. "Casey, please try to understand this one thing: what happened at your parents' house today was not your fault. There was no way that you could have known that it would happen and there's no way that you could have stopped it from happening. It was disgusting and upsetting and unpleasant and more than just a little frightening. But whatever else it may have been, within your control it was not."

Casey wanted more assurance, but opted out of yet another

chorus of the same tune. Instead, she reopened the night's earlier topic. "What happened to your dad and the house—after you found out what had been going on there, I mean."

"I had to all but threaten legal action to get him into one of the nursing homes in Janesville. They all handed me the usual line about waiting lists and power of attorney and compelling need and processing time for paperwork, etcetera, etcetera. When I finally told the last place that I would personally put down a six-month up-front payment, suddenly there was a room that had just become vacant and they would be oh so pleased to have Mr. Bingham as a resident."

"Was he happy there?"

"Who knows? The man couldn't recite the first four letters of the alphabet. He hated the diapers that they forced him to wear—of course, they didn't call them diapers, but that's exactly what they were. I know he really missed being out in the country. He had spent his whole life living in houses that were so isolated that you couldn't see another homestead from the windows. To go to a place like that must have felt like a prison sentence. Of course, the real incarceration was the lockdown in his brain."

"Did he know that he'd lost his mind, Kate?"

"I think he had better days where he'd have fleeting moments of knowing that he wasn't who he used to be, but for the most part, he was like a baby. No," Kate corrected herself, "he was more like a sweet, bumbling idiot or a semi-functional retarded person."

"So what about the house?"

"Once I got him checked into the home, I got a leave of absence from my job. I was just too embarrassed—more for him than for me—to have anyone else come into that house and clean it up. It warmed up to forty degrees or more the week after Thanksgiving, so I used the outside faucet and hosed out the cab and bed of his pickup. Most of the furniture was beyond salvage, so I dragged it by the truckload to the dump. Then I ripped up every single piece of floor covering in the place and hauled it off to the dump, too. After that, I scrubbed every wall and the bare floorboards with bleach and ammonia. And then I painted the whole place, top to bottom."

"Gawd, that must have been back-breaking. How could you manage it?"

"I was in pretty good shape back then—I worked out at the gym with weights, ran a couple of miles almost every day, did some yoga. Besides, I was a woman possessed. The sooner I could get it done, the sooner I could get back to Detroit" (to Nikki, she appended in her mind) "and finish getting ready to move to Connecticut."

"And Martha and Jolene . . . ?"

"Worthless as tits on a boar hog, as Dad used to say. They couldn't get so far as the front porch without starting to gag or swoon. Heaven forbid they risk breaking a nail themselves or ask their never-get-their-hands-dirty husbands to pitch in or to so much as offer a dime to repay me for the dump fees, cleaning supplies, and paint. Actually, it was sort of therapeutic to work like a longshoreman; it kept me from thinking about my dad. And working alone let me cry or scream or shout obscenities if I wanted to."

"Did you sell the house after you got it cleaned out?"

"No, as it turns out, the guy who had been renting the land—I think I told you that he was the son of one of our closest neighbors—had just gotten married. He found out that Dad was no longer living there and asked if he could rent the house, too, so that worked out really nicely."

Casey let the conversation lapse for a moment. "What was it like to go see your dad in the home?"

"Like ramming a hot poker in my eye. Every time I went, he had lost more ground. By the end, they had to tie him to the back of a chair if he was going to sit up without falling flat on his face."

"Sounds awful, Kate."

"It was, but remember, he had a true physical illness, not just Alzheimer's or some other mental disorder. I don't think your dad will have nearly as tough a run as Ray Bingham had."

"I hope you're right. But still—" Casey felt the tears burning at the back of her eyelids. Kate saw the first one fall from her lashes.

"Don't start," she admonished. "If you start, I'll be right behind you."

Without prompting, the cats and Roger leapt off the sofa and headed back for the bedroom. Casey and Kate crept toward the center of the sofa and wrapped around one another. Kate opened the throw so that it enfolded them both.

Together and yet alone, content with the silence and the occasional teardrop, they waited out the last hours of the night, each remembering the father who was now lost to her forever.

Chapter 16

"I've never seen her this bad this early in the day." Casey, Christine, and Kate were standing out on the deck of Burr and Nora's house. The sun was just barely making itself felt over the steep slant of the Carolina mountains. "I didn't expect her to be in the best of shape," Casey continued, "but she's absolutely drunk on her ass." She slapped her palms against her backside for emphasis.

"So she's been drinking more lately?" Christine asked with a hint of disbelief in her voice.

"Oh come on, Christine. I've been telling you for months that she's potted damn near every day. When are you going to take off your blinders and face up to what's going on here?"

"Well, don't get so high and mighty with me, Casey. You know that I only get up here from Florida a few times a year."

"Yeah, and I've been calling you every week with reports of Nora the lush and Burr the lunatic and you've been playing ostrich. Maybe now you'll finally pull your head out of the sand."

"You and Darren and Margie should have done something—"

"Oh, like Darren and Margie have been any more willing than you have to step in and figure out what to do." Casey shook her head, exasperated. "And by the way, just what is it that you think we should have done? Signed her up for Alcoholics Anonymous and enrolled Daddy in kindergarten for sexagenarians?"

"What does their sex life have to do with this?" Christine was obviously perplexed. "I mean just because of what we saw when we got here this morning . . ."

Casey shook her head again, this time in amusement. "A sexagenarian is someone in their sixties, you dope." She smiled at her older sister. "I'd offer to get you an unabridged lexicon for Christmas, but then you'd want to know why I won't let you take your fancy car across the river." The three women permitted themselves a moment's respite from the strain of what they had found when they had gotten to the house that morning.

Darren and Judy and Margie and Ed had loaded children into cars and headed back to Atlanta the previous evening as soon as it was clear that Kate and Casey would tend to Burr and Nora. Christine and Max and their daughter Angela had checked into a motel in Delano with nothing but what they were wearing at the time. Kate had, with their permission, stuffed most of what they had brought with them from Florida into trash bags and hauled it out of the house on her first pass at setting things right in the guest room that Burr had so thoroughly demolished the night before.

Kate and Casey were getting out of the Volvo just as Christine, Max, and Angela pulled into the yard. Christine had repeated her instructions to her husband about procuring enough clothes to get the three of them through a couple of days and back to Florida and then had leaned through the open rear window to give her daughter a kiss. Kate, Casey, and Christine braved the re-entry into Burr and Nora's world together.

It was only eight-thirty in the morning, but Nora was already incoherent and incapable of standing without help. When they walked through the front door, Burr was sitting on the loveseat in the living room wearing only an undershirt. On the coffee table in front of him were assorted unopened cans and a hand-crank can opener. The complexities of that high-tech device had completely baffled him. He had resorted to pulling the pop-top lids on cans of applesauce, pineapple, and beans and franks. He was using one hand to eat directly from the containers while he fingered his penis with the other hand.

They had gotten Burr dressed and fed him a somewhat more nourishing breakfast of toast, sausage, grits and coffee; they had put Nora into bed. Now Burr was sitting in front of the TV in the living room watching a cable channel that was broadcasting in French. Christine, Kate, and Casey opted for the deck to talk things over out of Burr's earshot but so that they could see him through the sliding glass door.

"So what now?" Christine asked, as much of the universe as a whole as of her two companions.

"I don't think there's much choice. He has to go to a home," Casey offered.

"He'll never consent to going to one of those places. You know that, Casey."

"We're not going to ask him if he wants to go. We're going to find a place and commit him. It's obvious that Mother can't be trusted to take care of him and even more obvious that he can't be left on his own."

"We can't just decide to do this. The others need to be part of this process."

"Oh for god's sake, Christine, do we need to go on the campaign trail and hold primaries and cast secret ballots and convene the Electoral College?"

"Casey." Kate spoke for the first time since the three of them had stepped outside. She touched Casey lightly on the arm. "I think that what she means is that your brothers and Margie need to help make this go as smoothly as possible for him. He's used to being the man in charge. It's not going to be easy for him to be stripped of his independence."

"I know that, Kate. But we don't have the luxury of shopping for just the right home and doing this in measured steps. Everybody's got jobs and kids and responsibilities. It's not like we can take turns babysitting him for a month at a time while we conduct research and do spreadsheets to analyze every nursing home in a hundred-mile radius."

Just then, Burr's voice boomed from the living room. He had managed to change the channel on the cable box and was tuned to a station that aired classic movies. The cowboy on the screen was strumming his guitar, seemingly singing to the herd of cattle superimposed (as best the technology of the medium permitted at that point in the evolution of the silver screen) onto the stage setting. Burr couldn't quite keep up with all the words of the song, but there was one phrase that he could unerringly belt out. The cowboy crooned, "Give me land, lots of land with the starry skies above . . ." Burr's version was something like "sandlots and skies and doves," but he chimed right in on the next line: "Don't fence me in!"

The poignancy of the sentiment was too much for the three conspirators watching through the glass door. They turned away from one another and from the cowboy who was about to have his spurs and bedroll stripped from him. Perhaps remembering the Biblical admonition about looking to the hills from whence cometh help, they stared off toward the mountains surrounding them.

Chapter 17

"No, Casey! I simply will not hear of it," Nora hissed through clenched teeth. She stomped her foot for emphasis and glowered at her daughter. Kate stood off to the side of the kitchen, leaning in the doorway to the main part of the house to keep one eye on Burr in the living room and one ear on the conversation between the two women.

It was the second weekend in December. The other Marsden siblings who had gathered for Thanksgiving had, for all apparent purposes, abdicated any responsibility for finding a suitable care facility for their father to Casey. When it became obvious that Darren, Christine, and Margie weren't going to provide any substantive help, Casey had made a couple of phone calls to the oldest of the bunch, her brother BJ, out in California to solicit his input. He was as distant emotionally as he was geographically and, like the others, proved eager to let Casey expend the energy, do the legwork, and make the decisions.

In the three weeks since Thanksgiving, Kate had taken several days of personal leave and had gone with Casey as she made the rounds to all of the nursing homes within striking distance of Delano. Although none of them was, as Casey put it, "the Hilton of old folks' homes," they had found a place sixty miles up the road in an outlying suburb of Asheville that had a special wing for the memory-impaired. Kate and Casey had gone back three times to watch the staff work with the residents. They seemed competent, compassionate, and patient as they dealt with old people who, due to strokes, accidents, Alzheimer's, or other causes, were more like poorly trained children than adults. Casey had completed the preliminary paperwork to have Burr admitted as a resident. Now the time had come to tell her parents of the plans for Burr to go to the Morning Sun Assisted Living Quarters.

Nora continued. "How dare you presume to know what's best for your father? How dare you do such a thing without consulting me? No, Casey. He is not going to one of those dreadful places. Not now. Not ever. Do you understand?" Nora paced the open area in the kitchen. She paused to look out the window over the sink and then turned and took several steps back so that she was directly in front of Casey. "He is my husband. I will take care of him."

"Mother, how can you take care of him? You can't even take care of yourself." Casey regretted the words as soon as they fell from her lips.

"And just what is that supposed to mean?" Nora's eyes flew open wide as she confronted her child.

"Look, Mother." Casey groped for the right thing to say. "It's just too much for you. He's really gone downhill a lot these past few months. It would be too much for anyone. We just want him to be someplace where he can get whatever medical attention he needs and where he can't wander off or get behind the wheel of the car and hurt himself or someone else."

"What medical care, Casey? He's not taking any prescriptions, and besides, there's nothing to treat what he has anyhow. He has never wandered off, and he won't as long as I'm here to watch him. As for the car, you don't think I'm capable of hiding the keys from him?"

"Actually, according to the doctors that I've talked to, there might be some drugs that could be of some help to him. You know that when I took him up to Asheville with me a few weeks ago, the doctor there confirmed that this is almost certainly Alzheimer's." Casey intentionally left Nora's other questions unanswered.

"Well, fine. Get him the medicine and that's that. He can take it right here at home." Nora dropped her shoulders slightly, the first brunt of her ire spent.

"It's more than that, Mother." Casey steeled herself and went on. "And you know it. There are lots of days when you're just not—um, just not—"

"Not *what*, Casey? For heaven's sake, just say what's on your mind and get it out in the open." Nora's fire was relit.

"Not quite yourself," Casey offered, lamely. "Not really at your best."

"What do you mean?" Nora's defenses were back on the rise. "How can I be at my best? My husband is losing his mind and I'm trapped here in a backwater mountain town without friends or entertainment. Shall I fry up some road kill and have the local idiots in for dinner and Crazy Eights?" Nora stepped briskly over to the tall hutch that stood on the wall adjoining the dining room. She opened the lower door and took out a bottle of scotch.

Casey glanced toward Kate for a boost of courage. Kate inclined her head ever so slightly in Nora's direction and cocked her eyebrow as if to say "now or never."

"That's what I mean, Mother. Some days, no, make that most days, you start drinking by midmorning, and by midafternoon, you're not really in control of yourself."

"So I have a little drink or two to help me cope with your father's incessant babbling and nattering." Nora went to the cupboard to retrieve a glass. "If you were cooped up in this house with him all day

97

every day, you'd want a little something to take the edge off, too." She splashed some liquor into the tumbler.

"Exactly what I was saying earlier. He needs to be in a home where trained caregivers can keep him occupied and so that you don't waste the rest of your life chasing after him."

"It is not a waste of my life taking care of the man I've been married to for more than forty years. It's not like it is with young people today or people like you and Kate who just call it quits when things get a little rough." She raised the glass and downed half of its contents in one gulp. "In my generation, and in a real marriage, we play for keeps." She drained the rest of the liquid and set the glass down on the counter with a flourish.

Both Kate and Casey knew this was not the time to take issue with Nora's sideways slap at their relationship and its prospects for longevity. Nonetheless, her remark caught them both off guard and left them hurt by the acrimony of her sentiment.

"And now, all this talk is giving me a headache. I think I need to take something." Nora started for the dining room, but Casey took two long strides and intercepted her before she could leave the kitchen. Her own indignation had been aggravated by her mother's callous comment and she used it to persevere with what she knew needed to be said.

"It's not just the booze, Mother. It's all the prescriptions you take. Either one alone would be bad enough, but together, you're an accident waiting to happen."

Nora wheeled on the balls of her feet and contorted her face into a scowl. "You're over the line, missy. I'm not going to have you come into my home and start making accusations like that. I am not some drug-abusing alcoholic. I'm doing the best I can in a very difficult situation. Instead of help and concern, all I get from you is finger pointing and disrespect. I won't have it, Casey. I simply won't have it."

As she surveyed the scene unfolding, for a moment, Kate was reminded of the Nora Marsden she had first known years earlier when they first worked together. If only that composed, no-nonsense version of Nora were still the one who showed up every day. Then Burr *would* be well cared for at home and everyone could have some peace of mind.

Nora stalked off through the dining room and down the hallway. Kate and Casey stood staring at one another, dumbstruck. Nora strode back into the room carrying as many pill bottles as she could hold in a precarious heap in her hands.

"Here, Casey. Since you think I'm just a pill-popping weakling, take these. It's every one I've got in the house." She dumped the hodgepodge of bottles onto the kitchen table and they clattered and rolled in every direction. "Pick those up," Nora commanded. Mutely, Casey complied and began stowing the vials in the pockets of her slacks and the fleece vest that she had hung over the back of one of the kitchen chairs when she and Kate had arrived less than twenty minutes earlier.

Nora went to the hutch and reopened the lower door. "While I'm at it, this goes, too." She snatched up assorted pints and fifths and set them in the sink. One by one, she removed the caps and poured the contents down the drain.

As the last of the booze gurgled away, Nora swiveled her head so that she was looking at Casey. "Now, if you don't mind, I'm going to fix some lunch for my husband and me. Forgive me for being rude, but I am very angry with you right now and I really would prefer that you leave my house." Nora exhaled sharply. She turned a little farther so that she was facing Kate. For the first time that morning, she acknowledged Kate's presence.

"Kate, I'm terribly sorry that you had to witness this unpleasantness. I'm sure Casey meant well in suggesting that her father be put away like your father was, but that's not how we do things here in the South." Nora cleared her throat before going on. "I know that you and Casey have become, uh, very close, and that's fine, but please don't go trying to force her into doing things your way. We're perfectly able to take care of our own in this family."

Kate was doubly thunderstruck. She had been wrong in her presumption that Nora knew nothing of her father's illness and his placement in a nursing home, and she was completely rocked on her heels by the vitriolic undertone of Nora's insinuations that it was her idea to look into a care facility for Burr. Casey, likewise shaken, took Kate by the elbow and steered her toward the front door. Kate mumbled something noncommittal to Nora and numbly slipped into her coat as she and Casey stepped out into the cool, crisp alpine air.

Nora followed them to the doorstep and let them get halfway down the walk before calling after them. "Oh, don't forget, girls, I'll need you both here next Saturday to help put up the tree and the other decorations."

Casey lifted an arm and gave a wave of concession as she and Kate got into the little red Nissan pickup. She started the engine and sat for a moment before rolling her head in Kate's direction.

"Too bad Rod Serling is dead." She punched the clutch and shoved the gearshift into reverse. "This would make a hell of a *Twilight Zone* episode."

Chapter 18

"Do you really think she's off the sauce for good?" Christine was sitting in the living room at Casey's house Tuesday afternoon, the day after Christmas. "I mean, she seemed just like the woman I used to know."

"To answer your question, no, I'm sorry to say, I don't think she's completely on the wagon." Casey kicked off her shoes as she drew her feet up into the seat of the chair and looked at her sister across from her on the sofa. "And I'm pretty sure she's gotten all her prescriptions refilled. I saw a bunch of bags from the pharmacy in the trash one day last week when I was over there helping her get ready for Christmas. She's just gotten a lot better at drinking on the sly and hiding the effects of the pills. I think she's just putting on a front all the time—sort of like she did when we first started noticing how bad Daddy was getting."

"Well, if what we saw over there yesterday is any indication, she should get an award for best supporting actress."

"Believe me, I know what you mean, Christine. Kate and I have been dropping in on them at every possible hour of the day and night, mostly to make sure that they're all right, but—I'm almost ashamed to admit it—also to see if we can catch Mother hitting the happy juice. Lots of times, we can smell the booze on her breath, but she always seems to be pretty much with the program. I guess all it took was the threat of putting him in a home to shape her up."

"Speaking of Kate, where is she?"

"She's working this week between Christmas and New Year's. She's taken so many days over the past month to help me with scoping out nursing homes that she was falling behind on some of her cases. She'll be up for the weekend."

"Well, I guess I won't get to see her again this trip since we're heading back to Florida tomorrow." Christine yawned and stretched her arms out to her sides. "You're taking BJ back to the airport, right?"

"Yeah. Mother insists that she and Daddy will ride along when we go on Thursday, but I really hope she changes her mind. It's almost three hours each way to the Atlanta airport from here. That's a long time to have him in such a confined place."

"Daddy does seem easily distracted, doesn't he?"

"Now there's an understatement," Casey derided. "Talk about adult attention deficit disorder."

"But you know, Casey, Mother seems to be handling it just fine."

"I guess. It all seems so strange, sis. Back in the fall, I'd have sworn she was almost as far gone as he was, but ever since she and I had that knock-down-drag-out over putting him in a home after that awful mess on Thanksgiving day, it's like she's operating from some completely neutral zone where nothing flaps her. And it all feels like a time warp, you know? I mean, it was just a month ago that we had to steam-clean the carpets in the guest room and . . ." Both sisters cringed at the recollection and were content to leave the details unrecounted.

"Well, who ever knows? I'm just glad that things are better."

Christine stood up and wandered over to the entertainment center. "It was nice to have everyone home again, huh?" She picked up a family photo from a Christmas gathering two years earlier. "Gosh, we've all changed a lot in a couple of years, haven't we? Look at how different, how much younger, both Mother and Daddy look in this picture." She walked back across the room and handed it to Casey.

"Uh-huh," she agreed as she took the frame. "I wonder how many more Christmases we'll have together?"

"As long as the folks kick in BJ's air fare, it'll go on forever." Christine was surprised at the catch in her voice as she replied. "It would have been nice if Darren and Margie and their families had hung around a little longer before racing back to Atlanta."

"Well, they're both strapped for cash, so they didn't want to spring for a motel for more than the one night. I'd have offered for them to stay here, but with you and Max and Angie camped in the second bedroom, that's all I can handle. After what happened at Mother's at Thanksgiving, who can blame them for not wanting to press their luck there? And BJ staying with them is all that they can cope with anyhow.

"Besides, all of the kids have got plans with friends and want to play with their Christmas junk, so I guess I understand why they all took off." Casey exhaled audibly. "Still, it would have been a big help if they could have taken BJ back down with them to save me all that chasing up and down the road."

"If you talk Mother into staying home with Daddy, couldn't you spend the night with Kate and just come back home the next morning?"

"Not really. I need to be here to take care of the animals—well, just Roger, really." Hearing his name mentioned, the dog roused himself from beside the sofa and nudged in next to Casey still curled in the easy chair. "It's kinda funny. I've only seen Kate's condo once. We went down to Atlanta one Saturday earlier this month to look for some Christmas gifts and we swung by there so that Kate could pick up a work file that she wanted to get."

"Was it nice?" Christine resumed her place on the sofa.

"Sure. She's got a good view of downtown Atlanta. The place is full of really nice furniture and really unusual oriental rugs and lots of really expensive pieces of artwork on the walls." Casey squinted before finishing her thought. "But then again, why shouldn't she have that sort of stuff? She makes more than six figures at Dewey Screwum and Howe. Makes my little cabin in the trees and hourly salary look kind of paltry."

"Are you two getting serious?"

"What's 'serious'?"

"Well, like you and Lindsay . . ."

Casey pondered before answering. "I'm pretty sure Lindsay was a once-in-a-lifetime deal." She craned her head to one side, shifted her feet to the floor, and went on. "As for Kate, we really haven't talked about what's next. Now that I think about it, it seems like most of our time together has been spent trying to figure out what to do about Mother and Daddy." She chuckled softly. "Real early on, Kate even accused Mother of trying to play matchmaker for her and me. Now there's a story line you wouldn't see on *The Brady Bunch*."

The Marsden girls engaged in a farcical rendition of the dialog that might have ensued between Marcia and Jan Brady had their mother interceded in setting one of them up with a potential lesbian love interest. By the time they were done, both were near tears with laughter.

They heard a car pull up on the gravel drive. "That'll be Max and the ankle biter back from exchanging the clothes that Mother bought them for Christmas," Christine conjectured.

"Ah, yes, the tradition lives on," Casey nodded. "It just wouldn't be Christmas without some inappropriate offering from Nora Marsden. I'll be making the same swap-off journey myself tomorrow after you guys hit the road."

Christine stood to go to the door to greet her husband and daughter. Casey rose at the same time, the family photo in her hand.

"As the TV commercial would say, celebrate the moments of

your life, little sister," Christine admonished as she glanced at the photo one more time.

As they caught one another's eye, the two fell into an embrace. Try as they might to stop them, the tears squeezed out of their eyes anyhow.

"Let me show you what I got," Angela declared as she bounded through the door.

Casey and Christine disentangled and turned to deal with the child before them. As though of a single mind, they both looked again at the picture Casey was still holding and simultaneously reached the same conclusion.

"She's a junior model of Mother," Christine averred.

"Spirit and image," Casey echoed.

Whatever other revelations and reflections that epiphany might have brought were lost in the excitement of inventorying the treasures from the cache of bags Angela dropped at their feet.

Chapter 19

"Happy almost New Year, Kate." Casey leaned over and kissed her on the temple. "Only two more hours till midnight."

"Same to you." Kate reached her hand to the far side of Casey's face and held Casey's cheek against her own. "I can't believe the Many Fortunes restaurant was open on New Year's Eve—a Sunday New Year's Eve, no less." She released Casey's face from her hand as she surveyed the empty cartons arrayed in front of them on the teak dining table in Casey's great room.

"As best I can tell, Many Fortunes is open twenty-four/seven. And the really amazing part is that no matter what day of the week you go in there or what time of the day or night, the same little oriental woman takes your order and the same little oriental man brings it out to the counter. I bet they don't even have a house or apartment—they probably sleep on bamboo mats in the kitchen."

"Well, whatever their living arrangements, they sure make a good kung pao." Kate fished a stray peanut out of the sauce left in one of the boxes. "Just hot enough and not too sweet."

"Speaking of sweet, you were an especially sweet lover in the bedroom earlier." Casey's voice came out soft and husky.

"I wanted to make up for having to rush off right after dinner on Christmas day. I hated leaving you, but I really needed to get back to Atlanta so that I could get to the office early the next morning."

"Chances are we would have been a little inhibited with my sister in the next room anyhow," Casey countered. "These walls aren't exactly soundproof."

"I guess Christine and Max got back to Florida all right?"

"Yep. She said the traffic was pretty decent. The worst of the Christmas crowd was already back home and the New Year's crowd hadn't hit the roadways yet."

"I suppose it sounds selfish, but I'm glad your family isn't getting together again tonight or tomorrow to ring out the old and ring in the new. We haven't had much time for just you and me in forever."

"I know." Casey lifted Kate's hand and brushed her lips across the knuckles. "Time was when we'd have had another big family dinner for New Year's, but Daddy barely got through Christmas without a meltdown. Everyone felt it was better to hang up a new calendar and let it go at that. Besides, with BJ and Christine already gone, at best, it would just be Darren and Margie with their families and us."

"And now that you mention BJ, I'm really sorry I couldn't spend some time with you on Thursday after you dropped him at the airport, but you know how crazy things are at the office."

"I know," Casey concurred. "Bernice told me you were in a meeting with the big guys." She lifted a forkful of foo young to her lips. "That woman has been a secretary at DS and H since Jesus wore diapers. She must be using a walker to get around by now."

"Hardly. I don't think Bernice is much older than I am. I know she was already working there when I first started in the Atlanta office way back when—probably started right out of secretarial school—but she's no more ancient than yours truly. She's one of the best secretaries I've ever had. And don't you doubt for a minute just how much clout she has in that office."

"So what sort of torture did Mr. DeWitt inflict on you?"

"Actually, it was all three of the partners. I'll tell you about it later." Kate started stacking plates and gathering trash. "First you tell me about what went on around here since I've been gone." She pushed back from the table and picked up the plates.

Casey grabbed glasses and serving spoons and followed Kate to the kitchen. "You already know most of it. Tuesday morning, Darren and Judy and Margie and Ed took appropriate children and went back to respective homes in Atlanta. Later in the day, Christine and Max and I—Angela, too, of course—went over to Mother's and hung out with my parents and BJ. Christine and Max left on Wednesday; then I took BJ back to the airport Thursday. Friday I did laundry and cleaned this place up a little." Casey gestured expansively with her arms, then rolled her eyes. "It would be a miracle if Christine even so much as stripped a bed." She put the utensils and dinnerware into the dishwasher. "And then, much to my delight, you were here by noon yesterday. So there"—she kissed Kate soundly—"you are now completely up to date."

They went back to the dining table and collected the last of the containers, napkins, and wrappers.

"Roger would probably like a chance to anoint the shrubs out back. Would you turn him loose while I finish up here?"

"Sure," Kate replied. "Come on, pooch, let's go scare the bears." Roger scampered to her side and accompanied her to the back door. "No, you're going by yourself, mister. I'll watch through the window," she scolded mockingly.

There was a heavy frost on the grass that prompted the dog to make short work of his outdoor business. Kate wiped his feet with a towel for that purpose from atop the dryer. When she rejoined Casey in the great room, the CD player was putting out soothing tunes and Casey was just finishing adjusting the dimmer switch.

"Hello, sailor. Can I buy you a drink?" Casey pulled a bottle of white wine from the small rack next to the entertainment center. "I guess I should have gotten some champagne. Just wasn't thinking, I guess."

"No, wine is fine, babe. Champagne always gives me a headache."

Casey uncorked the bottle, took two stemmed flutes from the slotted holder incorporated into the entertainment center, and poured a glass for each of them.

"Here you go." She handed Kate her glass. They drifted to the sofa and sat down close to one another.

"You didn't say much about how your mom and dad are doing, Casey. What sort of week have they had?"

"Well, you know that the turmoil of having all those people in the house usually just unhinges Daddy, but he did pretty well all week. I think Mother probably has been giving him some of her tranquilizers. Didn't you think he was remarkably subdued Christmas day?"

"Yes, he did seem awfully calm. But I thought your mother ditched all her drugs that day we were over there to tell her we were putting your dad in the home. What was the name of that place? Oh, yeah, Morning Sun," Kate concluded, answering her own question.

"She wants us to think she's off the poppers, but I'm pretty sure she's had every one of them renewed. She's doing a much better job of squirreling them away. And don't think I haven't gone looking."

"You know, there's something I've been meaning to ask you for weeks now, but there never seemed to be an opportunity to do it."

"What's that, Kate?"

"That Saturday we went over there and dropped the bomb about the nursing home, first she sort of suggested that she thought you and I—well, all lesbians, I guess—just play house and don't know how to build a real relationship. And then not five minutes later, she came out with some really ugly things about how it was wrong to have put my dad in a home and about how I was putting undue influence on you to do the same for your dad. What was up with that?"

"For as much time as you've spent around her, you haven't done a very good job of recognizing her defense maneuvers, have you?"

"Meaning . . . ?" Kate queried.

"Meaning that if she can get you rattled by a seemingly apropos but disturbing comment, you're less likely to be able to focus on whatever the topic at hand is. She's used that ploy for as long as I can remember, especially if she feels like she's being accused of not fulfilling what's expected of her. If I remember the conversation, she even lobbed in the old stand-by line of 'here in the South,' or some such."

"Yeah, I seem to recall that, too," Kate concurred.

"I don't really expect you to understand because you're not from here," Casey cast a teasing grin as she added, "you carpetbagger," then continued more seriously, "but women raised in the South have this thing about standing by their man and defending him through thick and thin, even if it means lashing out at someone who's been a friend for years and years. She didn't really mean to hurt your feelings. She just wanted to get the spotlight off her."

Kate furrowed her forehead as she mulled Casey's explanation. "I don't think that's exclusively a trait that Southern women can claim. Nobody likes to feel like they're being called incompetent or out of control."

"Maybe so, but it's an art form down here. And unless I miss my guess, you'll see my mother display it more and more frequently as this state of affairs with Daddy plays out."

"Well thanks for the crash course on reading your mother. Anyway, how did she hold up this week?"

"Oh she's always put on a big show for BJ whenever he's come home. We're all convinced he's her favorite child. She was the perfect Southern matriarch the whole time he was here."

"I'm sorry I didn't get to spend more time with him. I was in and out of there so fast on Christmas day I hardly felt like I got to meet him. I don't think I remember him uttering two sentences in the course of the meal."

"Don't feel rained on. I had him in Mother's car with me for the drive back to the airport for three hours on Thursday and other than 'Does this thing have any heat?' or 'Pick a different radio station,' he didn't have much to say to me either."

"So what's the deal with him? Does he talk to Darren? Or how about your dad? Well, I mean, did he used to when your dad could still hold up half of a conversation?"

"You've got to be kidding," Casey derided. "Dad all but disowned him when he moved to California, and Darren is much too macho for anyone's good."

"I don't think I get it, Casey."

"Oh, lordy, Kate. Do I need to paint you a picture? No wait, I should have BJ paint it for you. He's the artist after all."

"Well, he is, isn't he?"

Casey looked intently at Kate before replying, "He is. And he is also one of the biggest flamers in the Castro. Surely you figured out that he's gay . . ."

Kate pulled her head back as though someone had her neck on a string.

"No joke?"

"Pick your face up out of your abacus, darling. How could you miss it? The feathers were fairly flying from his boa."

"Well, I just thought he was really campy or just kind of— hmmm—delicate," she finished faintly. "Your dad doesn't approve? I thought he was OK with gays."

"I can't really explain it, but for some reason my being lesbian was OK, but BJ's being homosexual wasn't. Oh, I don't know." Casey wagged her head from side to side. "Maybe it's got something to do with carrying on the family name or some male bonding thing or the age-old crap about feeling threatened by it. When BJ came out, Daddy pretty much threw him out of the house. It was a good thing he wanted to move to San Francisco, because Burleson Marsden sure as heck didn't want a queer son anywhere near him."

"And Darren?"

"Same song, different generation. Darren always takes his cue from Daddy. If Daddy said pigs flew, Darren bought stock in porker airlines."

"So what happened? I mean, BJ still comes home. Your parents buy his plane tickets. Things must have gotten better between your dad and BJ."

"Not really. Before Daddy got sick, BJ would still come home, but Mother funded the air fare and he'd come back to see her. Daddy would just ignore him while he was home. Then, when Daddy started slipping mentally, it sort of became a non-issue. It's a shame really, because now there's no hope of the two of them ever making peace."

"What's the deal with Darren? Like I said, I didn't get to spend much time with everyone at Christmas, but there didn't seem to be any hostility between him and BJ."

"It's all part of what I fondly refer to as my family's Tennessee Williams syndrome. Daddy always thought he was the boss, but Mother really ran the show."

"But I thought you told me once that your father was all but a tyrant," Kate interjected. "And I know your mother was really unhappy with his unilateral decision that they were moving up here instead of building their retirement home on Lake Lanier."

"Oh, for the really big things, like where we lived and whether it was time for a new car and where money got invested and stuff like that, Daddy was a one-vote dictator. But for everything else, my mother ruled with an iron fist in a velvet glove. She got her way almost all the time. She just did it in such a way that everyone still saw her as the poor martyred mama. Trust me when I say no one ever dared cross her when it came to her children. And BJ was her firstborn . . . a boy child, no less. What is it with mothers and sons, anyway? He's always been her darling. Like you said, he *is* delicate. Always has been. He had lots of health problems when he was little, stuff like that. Mother has always protected him. I'd bet you anything she still sends him money on a regular basis."

"Huh. Well, I can see I should have stuck around for the second act instead of charging home to Atlanta. When do you think BJ will be back? I'd like to get to know him better."

"I wouldn't look for him till next Christmas. He's out of his element when he's here. Just because folks share a gene pool doesn't mean they have much in common."

"Tell me about it. My Christmas cards from my sisters this year had pre-stamped signatures in gold letters. Not a single handwritten word from either one of them. Not even a copy of the canned universal typed letter that I know they put in the cards they send to their friends and our aunts and uncles."

"Families." Casey sighed. "What a concept, eh, Kate?" Casey moved even closer to Kate and hugged her briefly. "I'm glad to have you to bring in the new year with."

"Me, too. I'd like some more wine. How about you?"

"Just a half glass, please."

Kate got to her feet and refilled the stemware. She took a deep breath as she returned to the sofa and offered Casey her glass.

"Since we're on the topic of families, there's something I want to ask you about." She paused only a second before blurting out what she had been rehearsing in her mind for the past three days. "How would you feel about moving to Connecticut?"

The question was so far from anything that Casey could have conjured that she dropped her jaw and then dropped her wineglass.

Chapter 20

"Connecticut," Casey repeated yet again as she used a dishtowel to wick up the spilled wine from the stain-repellant surface of the sofa. Kate was on the floor with one of the clean dog towels from the utility room sponging the wine from the area rug under the coffee table.

"It's part of the continental United States, Casey. Up the East Coast—New England."

"I know that, Kate, but why in the world would you want to move back to Connecticut? I thought you'd only just gotten back down here earlier this year."

"Let me put these out in the laundry basket and then I'll explain." Kate scooped up the damp towels and Casey's dropped glass. She set the glass in the sink and took the towels to the washing machine in the adjacent room. She grabbed the wine bottle and a fresh glass for Casey from the entertainment center on her way back to the sofa.

"OK, here's the deal. On Thursday, the partners called me into the boardroom. Actually, I knew about the meeting on Wednesday, but I didn't say anything to you when we talked Wednesday evening because I didn't know for sure what it was all about." Kate clasped and unclasped her hands in front of her. "They want me to move back to New Haven to be the head accountant in that office." She waited for the congratulatory cheer that she was sure Casey would produce. It didn't come.

"And you told them you would?" Casey's tone was somewhere between shell-shocked incredulity and accusatory disbelief.

"Well, no, not definitively. But why wouldn't I?" Kate could tell from the look on Casey's face that she failed to see the conspicuous desirability of the opportunity. "Casey, heading up a whole office like New Haven is an obvious step toward partnership in the firm." Kate sounded as though she were explaining the notion of using buttons and buttonholes to a toddler just learning to dress herself. "If I do a good job with that, I'm all but guaranteed a shot for at least junior partnership."

"And that's what you want?"

"I've been working at DS and H for over twenty years. I've got a good reputation and a lot of first-rate experience. I'll probably work another twenty years. Of course I want to keep getting promotions and moving up in the organization. What's the point of getting up every day and grinding all those numbers for all those clients if you're not going to have something to show for it when it's done?"

Casey tried to wrap her mind around what Kate was telling her. She tried to picture herself packing up the things in her house and locking the door for the last time as she left for New Haven, Connecticut. It wouldn't come into focus. Then she tried to picture herself sitting in her house—on that very sofa in that very great room—without Kate there, too. That was an even more blurry picture, probably due to the tears that were streaming down her face.

"Gosh, Casey. I didn't think you'd take it like this. What's wrong?"

"Gee, let me see. Oh, yes, my father is crackers, my mother, who has been working up to quite a dependency on alcohol and prescription medicine, is now turning into a closet drinker, my brothers and sisters are perfectly content to hide in Never-Never Land and let me deal with the aforementioned parents all by myself, I am at least three months away from my next paycheck and the cash reserves are shrinking fast, and hmmm . . ." Casey tapped her forehead as though concentrating. "Ah, that's right. The woman I was just starting to count on as the central player in my life has just told me she's moving a thousand miles away. Other than that, I can't think of a single thing to be upset about." She pulled a tissue from the pocket of her sweatpants and blew her nose.

Kate cocked herself sideways on the sofa so that she could look directly at Casey. "Didn't you hear what I said at the beginning of this conversation?" She waited for a reply; none was forthcoming. "I asked how you'd feel about moving to Connecticut. I want you to come with me, babe."

"And didn't you hear what I just said?" Casey asked, stern-faced. "I can't just up and run from here. Who's going to take care of my mother and father?"

"Margie is only two hours from here and Darren only slightly farther than that. Why can't they work out some sort of schedule to check on them once a week or something? Besides, your mom is doing a whole lot better. For the most part, she can do whatever needs doing for your dad." Kate didn't wait for Casey to offer counterarguments. "And we wouldn't be gone forever. It would be two years, tops, in New Haven. The home office is in Atlanta. When they offer me the junior partnership, I'm sure I'll be right back here. Well, there—I mean here—oh, you know what I mean."

Casey hopped off the sofa and flung her hands in the air. "Kate, two years in my dad's life is like a century. Look how much worse he's gotten just between when you first came up here in September and now. In two years, who knows how bad it will be."

"And he might stay about like he is for eighteen months, too.

116

Nobody's crystal ball can say just what will happen. You can't put your life on hold simply because something unpleasant might come along."

"I can't believe you!" Casey flared. "It's not like everything is peachy fine wonderful here in the mountains of western Carolina and we're just going off on a little vacation. We already know there's trouble, and I mean big trouble, with Daddy and probably just as big a problem on the horizon for Mother. Leaving now would be just like pouring gasoline all over their house, leaving lighters lying around everywhere, and telling the fire department not to bother coming by if someone mentions that their house is blazing out of control." Casey circled the back of the sofa and angrily pressed the power button on the CD player. "Not much in the mood for music," she grunted, by way of explanation.

"Well, what about my going to Connecticut alone?" Kate posed the question hesitantly.

"What about it? I certainly couldn't stop you."

Kate rose from the sofa and walked around it to where Casey was standing.

"This isn't how I wanted tonight to go, Casey." Kate's manner was conciliatory.

Casey met Kate's gaze in the soft light from the hanging lamp. "Wouldn't have been my first choice either, Kate." She pulled in a breath. "But here we are." Her lower lip quivered.

"I got all caught up in myself and I didn't think this through very carefully. I was just so excited about the offer from DS and H, and I thought that since your mom has seemed so much better these past few weeks that we could just make a brand-new start in a brand-new year. I'm sorry, sweetest, I guess I thought you felt about me like I feel about you."

"Huh?" Casey seemed genuinely bewildered.

Kate reached out and drew Casey nearer to her. "I'm crazy about you, Ms. Marsden. Have been for months. I adore being with you; I hate being away from you. I want you with me every day. I want you beside me in bed every night. This New Haven thing seemed like the perfect way to make all that come true." She pulled Casey tightly to her body. "I love you, Casey." Her lips were close to Casey's ear. The last words were little more than a whisper.

"That's the problem, dammit." Casey started to cry again. "I love you, too. My least favorite thing is watching you pull out of here to go back to Atlanta. During the day, I can stay busy with running errands for Mother or giving her a break from dealing with Daddy or messing around with projects here at the house, but weeknights when you're not here, I feel like I'm going to just go insane from missing you." She rocked the two of them from side to side.

"You love me?" Kate's question was sincere. She stepped back slightly so that she could see Casey's face.

"Well, duh." Casey couldn't resist the chance to tease a little.

"No, be serious. Really?"

"Really, Kate. I've wanted to say it to you for what feels like forever, but . . ."

"But what?"

"But I was afraid you wouldn't say it back." She took Kate's hand and led her to the front of the sofa. "Remember how we sat up talking Thanksgiving night after that nightmare at Mother's?" Kate nodded. "You said you were falling in love with me. That was the first time you'd said anything like that."

Kate grinned wryly. "Gun shy, I guess. I was sure I'd spend the rest of my life alone. Not to mention that I had promised myself I wasn't going to hang my heart out on the line to have it get shot all to pieces again." She smiled broadly. "I hadn't counted on finding you."

"Look." Casey pointed toward the clock on the bookcase. "It's less than a half hour till midnight."

"I have a suggestion. How about we declare 'time out' from this discussion and watch the giant peach drop from the tower at Underground?"

"Yeah, I think we should," Casey agreed. "Let's use the little TV in the bedroom, OK?"

Without another word, the two women made their way down the hall and slipped out of their clothes and under the covers. The cats, already in their accustomed spot at the foot of the bed, and Roger, curled in a tight ball in his bed in the corner, barely lifted their eyelids. Casey hit the power button on the remote and flipped to a channel covering the New Year's Eve celebration in downtown Atlanta.

"Oh, I forgot the wine." Casey made a move to get up.

"Don't bother, babe. We can get some later if we want it." Kate kissed her gently. "Now, tell me again what you told me out in the great room a little while ago."

"What?" Casey feigned ignorance.

"Repeat after me," Kate encouraged as she rolled so that she was in full frontal contact with the woman beside her. "I love you."

"I love you. I love you. I love you." Momentary hesitation. "Let me show you."

Watching a brightly lit fake fruit slide down a metal structure while a giant clock ticked off seconds in the background wasn't really all that entertaining after all.

Chapter 21

"Should I open another one?" Casey tilted the empty wine bottle and held it out toward Kate.

"No, not on my account. Help yourself, though."

"I'd be just as happy with a Coke." Casey boosted herself from the easy chair and started for the kitchen. "Want one?" she asked over her shoulder.

"Huh-uh. I'll have to make six trips to the bathroom between now and daylight as it is." Kate looked at the clock as Casey left the room. It was one-thirty in the morning, New Year's Day.

Casey returned shortly with her soft drink. "So, much as I probably don't want to hear about it, tell me the rest of the story about New Haven," she invited as she sat down. Kate was on the sofa, diagonally opposite her, across the coffee table.

"The person in charge of the New Haven office—a man, I might add, which happens to be the same gender of every other person in charge of any of DS and H's field offices—is retiring the end of June. Since I worked up there for almost seven years, Mr. Hastings—that's his name—got to know me pretty well. According to what they told me in the meeting on Thursday, Hastings personally recommended me to be his successor in New Haven. Mr. Howell told me that Mr. Hastings hadn't wanted me to leave the New Haven office back in June, but then he decided that it would be a good thing for the big cheeses in Atlanta to have me right under their noses so that when he told them he wanted me to take over behind him they'd be reminded of what a good choice I'd be." Kate collected her thoughts before continuing.

"I wouldn't have to go right away, Casey. As long as I'm up there in time to do a transition with him, say a month or so, that would be all I'd need. That would give us till Memorial Day to get things squared away down here." She waited for Casey to grab the thread and tug.

"Memorial Day, Fourth of July, Labor Day, Halloween, next Thanksgiving." Casey ticked each one off on her fingers as she spoke. "It doesn't matter 'when,' Kate. It's the 'what' that I can't get past."

"Your parents." It was half question, half statement.

"Yes, that's certainly the biggest part of it, but it's more than that."

"I'm listening," Kate prodded.

"I like it here. I like my house. I love working at the nursery, even if it does leave me without an income for the winter months. I did the Atlanta thing for years, and I've had my fill of the crowds and traffic and noise and hassles. I just can't see myself ever living in a big city, well, hell, in any city for that matter, ever again."

"But New Haven is really pretty. It sits right on Long Island Sound. We could get a condo overlooking the water."

"If my memory of U.S. geography serves me, it also sits about halfway between New York on one side and Boston on the other. You might just as well get me a jacket with buckles on the sleeves and an oil tanker full of Prozac. I hyperventilate just thinking about it."

121

Roger trotted into the great room from the hallway to the bedrooms and did his circle dance indicating a need to go outside.

Casey stood to accompany him to the back door. "And what about this little guy?" She rubbed his head as she spoke. "How do you think he'd do in an oceanfront condominium?" Before Kate could speak, Casey and the dog were out of the room.

Kate waited several minutes, sure that Casey would return as soon as Roger had emptied his bladder. When they didn't show, she walked through the kitchen and the utility room to the back door. Casey was looking out the window in the top half of the door into the small part of the yard behind the house. The fixture by the back door cast its light almost to the woods fifty feet beyond the house. She turned as she heard Kate approach.

"Look at him," she suggested as Kate slipped an arm around her waist. Roger was patrolling with his nose barely off the ground. "He knows what every inch of this yard is supposed to smell like." Casey coughed and went on. "You know that he was abused, right? The people who had him tied him to a stake in a dirt yard on a chain about three feet long. They fed him maybe once a week. And just for sport, they kicked him in the ribs so hard that it broke several of them." Casey sniffed as she fought the tears. "One of the neighbors called the county animal shelter and they came and cut him loose from the chain and took him in. Turns out, it was the very next day that I went to the shelter looking for a furry kid."

Casey had to wait for the lump in her throat to shrink before she could say anything more. "I was just going to get one cat—something warm to sit in my lap that I could talk to when I felt like it and ignore most of the rest of the time. I had all but made up my mind to adopt a little calico kitten when this lady walked into the shelter carrying two cats in a carrier. She told the woman at the desk that the cats belonged to her sister and that her sister had just died of breast cancer and that there was no one to take care of the cats and—" Casey's voice gave way completely and she laid her head on Kate's shoulder and sobbed quietly.

As she regained her composure, she continued. "The woman said she didn't even know what the cats' names were. She had just flown in from Oregon to be there to help with her sister's last days and make the funeral arrangements. She said she'd just loaded up the cats to bring them in and had gathered up everything that looked like it was cat stuff. Can you guess the expression she used?"

"The whole kit and caboodle?" Kate ventured.

"Bingo," Casey affirmed. "How could I not take them? It was like Lindsay was right there with me saying, 'Hey, kid, here's a chance to do something to help put the karmic scales back in balance.' Well, heck. The kitten was so tiny and cute that she at least stood a chance of still finding a home, but with all the animals already crowding the cages, these two grown cats would have been next in line for the needle."

"And Roger?" Kate nudged.

"While I was quizzing the woman who had brought Kit and Caboodle in for whatever details she could give me and sorting through the toys and litter pans and bags of food she had carted along, the woman at the desk started telling us about the dog that they had rescued the night before. She said that they weren't sure that he'd make it because he was so malnourished and so badly beaten.

"I don't know where the words came from, but the next sound I heard was my own voice saying I wanted to see him. As you can surmise, it was love at first sight. He was so pitiful, Kate. My first impression was that all there was to him was skin, bones, ears, and eyes—those big, brown, pleading eyes."

"And—?"

"And many trips to the vet and many dollars and many cans of Alpo later, he rallied to become the speeding bullet you see before you now." Roger raced past the stoop in pursuit of something only he could see in the peculiar yellow light that the bug-deterrent bulb cast.

"So how did you decide to call him Roger?"

"When the worker at the shelter took me back to see him in his crate, she kept saying, 'It could be game over and lights out for this one.' It reminded me of the old movies where the fighter pilots always said, 'Roger, over and out,' when they talked on their radios. I knew the minute I laid eyes on him I didn't want it to be over and out, so I picked 'Roger' instead." They watched the dog who seemed to have long forgotten his difficult early days thunder past the door one more time. "Dumb, huh?"

"Not at all, Mama. I think it's very sweet." She gave Casey a soulful kiss to underscore the judgment.

Suddenly it occurred to the dog that his two favorite people were at the door and that he could surrender his game of solo tag. Casey cracked the door and Roger wiggled inside and sat on the rug waiting for the inevitable foot wiping with a towel.

Casey dropped to the floor to give each paw a swipe. "The cats would adjust, I guess, but I can't do it to him, Kate." Casey stood up. "He was a throw-away dog once already. I won't throw him away again, and he wouldn't be happy looking out the window at pounding surf. He needs the freedom to run. He's a mountain dweller. A Southerner."

Casey dropped her voice. "And so am I."

Chapter 22

As they had Thanksgiving night, Kate and Casey decided that a few hours' sleep would be more damaging than none, so they sat up for the remainder of the night and talked. New Year's Day dawned gray and drizzly. The thermometer hovered at thirty-four degrees, making both of them nervous about Kate's impending drive back to Atlanta over potentially slick roads.

If the definition of insanity is doing the same thing over and over again thinking that there will be a different outcome, then, by the time Kate tossed her few possessions into the tote bag she used for her weekend visits to Casey's, they both were certifiable. Kate tried every angle she could think of to get Casey to see that a move to Connecticut was a workable, positive thing. For her part, Casey parried every thrust with the same negative reply. Neither woman expressed any anger, but certainly sadness and disappointment crept in a little deeper each time they reworked the tired script.

Late in the forenoon, they turned on the television in the great room to catch some of the Rose Bowl parade and to check out some of the pre-game coverage. All of the Atlanta network stations were running tickers on the bottom of the screen forecasting the dreaded "wintry mix" of rain, sleet, snow, and freezing rain for all of the broadcast vicinity.

"Guess I'd better go." Kate was feeling the effects of too much wine, too little sleep, and too much conversation without resolution.

"You're sure you can't stay? The weather is supposed to clear up by afternoon tomorrow."

"Darling Casey," Kate sighed, "I work for an accounting firm. Tomorrow marks the official start of the Maalox season for every CPA in the country. My calendar is absolutely packed. If I fall behind by one day this early in the filing season I may as well plan on being behind right up until midnight April fifteenth." She wrapped her arms around Casey. "I wish I could stay, you know that, but I can't." Kate dropped her tote bag and briefcase on the floor and opened the door to the small closet by the front door. She took her coat off its hanger and pulled her gloves from the pockets. "Let me go tell the kids good-bye."

Kate walked quickly to the bedroom where she was sure the cats would be snoozing on the people bed and Roger would be nestled in his doggie bed. She stroked each one in turn. "You're pretty lucky little critters, you know," she said softly to the threesome. "You've got one of the most tender-hearted mamas in the world." She was surprised at how much emotion welled in her as she looked at the contented creatures in the room where she had found so much happiness with their owner.

"Keep an eye on her for me, OK, guys? I love her, and she says she loves me, too. How about that?" With one last nuzzle for each pet she was on her way.

"I almost forgot to give you this." Casey offered a small wooden framed picture to Kate as she came back into the great room.

"What's this?" Kate asked before looking at the photo it contained.

"Christine had a couple of frames left on the roll of film in her

126

camera and she wanted to get the pictures developed before they went back to Florida, so she took this one of me and the menagerie to finish up the roll."

The snapshot showed Casey sitting on the sofa with Roger crouched on his haunches on the floor in front of her and Kit draped across her lap while Caboodle lolled next to her right thigh.

"Wow! What a great family shot. Thanks, Casey." Kate plopped a kiss on her cheek.

"Christine got double prints, so I've got one just like it. I stuck it in the drawer over here." Casey stepped over to the entertainment center and pulled her matching frame out and set it down next to the picture of the Marsdens at Christmas two year ago that she and Christine had looked at just a few days earlier.

"It is a pretty good likeness of all of us, isn't it?" Casey gestured toward the photo as she retraced her steps back to Kate still standing by the front door. "You know what would make it even better?"

"I can't imagine. It looks fine to me." Kate intensified her gaze to try to find the flaw.

"If you were in it, too, then it would be perfect." Casey knew better than to say it, but she seemed powerless to stop herself. "About New Haven . . ."

Kate laid a finger across Casey's lips. "Don't. We can't drag ourselves through that again. Nothing has changed in the last hour. I've got to go before the roads ice up." She slipped the frame into the tote bag as she reclaimed it from the floor.

She saw Casey's face fall. "Nothing is carved in stone yet, love. Let's both just give ourselves some time to think about all of the options and we'll talk when I come back next weekend." She leaned in get her farewell kiss. "There's just got to be a way to work this out. I can't stand saying good-bye to you every weekend."

Casey walked with her to the car and stood atop the hill and waved as Kate made her way out of the yard. As always, Kate flicked the lights on and off twice in rapid succession just before she was beyond the point where she could still see Casey in the rearview.

Once far enough down the road that she was sure Casey had gone back into the warmth of the house, Kate edged the Volvo to the side of the road and set the parking brake. She reached into the back seat and drew the photo of Casey and the kids out of the tote bag.

"Now what?" she asked of the images in the picture. "I can have you, or I can have my job." She pulled the ashtray open and propped the frame between the open edge of it and the dashboard. "How in the name of all that's holy am I supposed to make a choice like that?"

With a shake of her head, Kate pushed the question out of her mind and followed the road back to Atlanta and the start of the busiest three and a half months of her year.

Chapter 23

"Oh, thank God! I've been calling your place for the past two hours. I was afraid you were in the ditch down on Highway 365 someplace."

"I know. I just erased your seven messages from the answering machine." Kate kicked off her shoes and pushed the up arrow on the digital thermostat. "I just this minute came through the door. I tried calling you on my cell phone the whole trip down, but the weather must be blocking out the signals."

"Did you have bad roads?"

"Not really. There were a couple of patches where I think there might have been some black ice, but Ole and Sven did a pretty good job of engineering a sure-footed vehicle and I've got almost new tires, so we did OK. The traffic was really, really heavy, though. It is New Year's Day, after all, and lots of folks are trying to get back home after the holidays. I suspect the crappy weather chased people onto the highways earlier than they might otherwise have gone."

"What took you so long to get home? You left here almost four hours ago."

"For one thing, I drove a lot slower for the first thirty miles or so till I got out of the mountains. Then there was a wreck on Highway 441 at the traffic light in Clayton. It was just a fender bender, but the sheriff and his boys were having a devil of a time getting it out of the middle of the road. The real hangup, though, was a dozen or so clowns decided to play bumper cars right at Spaghetti Junction. You know what a jumble that is anyway where I-85 hooks up with the Perimeter. Well, with the rain and the extra traffic, it was pure grid-lock. I sat in the backup for over forty-five minutes without moving an inch."

"Sorry for the problems, Kate. I'm glad you're safe."

"Thanks. Me, too. And it's hardly yours to apologize for. You didn't make these nutcases act like eighty-five is the mandatory min-imum speed as opposed to the road number." Kate shifted the portable phone from ear to ear as she shimmied out of her clothes and into baggy sweats while they talked. "You sound funny—all stuffed up or something. Are you OK?"

"Not really."

"Have you been crying? It's not still the New Haven thing, is it? We said we'd talk about it next weekend."

"No, that's not it. Well, it sort of is, but I really haven't had much chance to think about that since you left."

"What then?"

"Since it looks like we might be in for a day or two of closed roads, I decided I should run over to check on Mother and Daddy to be sure they had everything they might need and to say 'Happy New Year's.' It was probably about one o'clock when I got there." Kate waited for her to continue. "Casey? You still there?"

"Sorry. Yes, I'm here. Oh, Kate," she sighed, "it was like the past couple of weeks were all just a fairy tale. Mother was schnockered and Daddy had pulled every single bag, can, and box out of every cupboard in the kitchen. He had torn things open and eaten everything from cake mix to marshmallows to beef broth."

"Oh, gawd! Please don't tell me he got sick again."

"No, no. Nothing like that. He just ate a bite or two of anything he could open and since nothing tasted good, he'd move on to the next thing. The kitchen looked like the scene of a fraternity food fight."

"Where was your mom?"

"In the small bedroom at the back of the house. The room she calls her sewing room."

"What was she doing?"

"Well, when I got there, she was sitting on the daybed with all the jars of the kids' finger paints spread around her. She had used them to create all sorts of abstract designs on the cream-colored quilt on top of the daybed. It was obvious that before I got there, she had consumed an awful lot of liquor and probably helped the cause with some legal mood-altering substances."

"I don't suppose you found out where she's keeping her pills now," Kate pressed. She sat in her darkened living room, looking out the picture window toward the illuminated skyline of downtown Atlanta.

Casey gave a half-laugh. "Did you ever read 'The Purloined Letter'?"

"Wasn't that a short story by Edgar Allan Poe?" Kate asked, bewildered. "What a bizarre question."

"Not really. Do you remember where the letter was hidden?"

"Gosh, Casey. I probably read that story in eighth grade. No, I can't say as though I recall the details."

"It wasn't hidden at all. The letter was right on top of the desk in a stack of other letters."

"And tell me again, just why is this relevant to your mother's stockpile of medications?" Kate was losing her patience.

"I told you I'd done some looking around trying to find where she was hiding them, right?"

"Uh-huh. We talked about that just last night."

"They're right where they always were."

"In the medicine cabinet in the hall bath and her nightstand?" Kate propounded.

"Right," Casey confirmed. "When I first knew about the assorted prescriptions she had in the house, I remember asking Mother if she didn't think it was risky to have them where Daddy could get to them so easily. She told me that he never sets foot in the hall bath. She thought it was because the sink and commode are in opposite positions from where they are in the bathroom off their bedroom and it confuses him. Anyway, she also told me that right from the early days of their marriage, one of their rules was that they couldn't look in one another's nightstands. I think it's where they used to hide little presents for one another back when they still did romantic stuff like that."

"Well, surely you would have looked in those places when you went rummaging for them last week or whenever." Kate was still perplexed by the unfolding story.

"Of course I did, and what I found in the medicine cabinet was a bottle of antacids, a bottle of low-dose aspirin, a bottle of regular aspirin, a box of Band-Aids, a package of corn pads, all the usual stuff. And in the nightstand, there was a box of cough drops, a metal box of throat lozenges, a little flashlight—nothing out of the ordinary."

"Casey—" Kate's vexation was showing.

"She had emptied all of the boxes and bottles and packages and put her drugs in them. She had even stuffed them with cotton balls or crumpled pieces of paper to keep them from sounding funny if you shook them."

"Pretty clever of her. What tipped you off?"

"By the time I got over there this afternoon, I was already working on the start of a headache."

"Yeah, I had one, too. Probably the wine and the lack of sleep and the not-so-happy conversations we had all night," Kate reflected.

"Then when I found out that I had returned to the *House of Usher*—"

Kate butted in before Casey could finish her sentence. "You really were a big fan of Poe, weren't you?"

Casey chuckled softly when she realized Kate's reference. "Well, I did minor in English literature. Sorry. Just a coincidence. But what I was saying was that as soon as I saw what was going on at my parents' house, my headache went from a three to an eleven on a ten-point scale and I went to get something to take. Imagine my delight to find that nothing in the medicine cabinet was what the label said. At least she had put pieces of paper in with each kind of pills so that she could tell what was what."

"Same deal with the flashlight and cough drop box in the nightstand?"

"You got it, Sherlock."

"I take it you're calling me from their house?"

"No. I was so furious with my mother that I just wanted to get out of there."

"Gee, Casey, do you think it was a good thing to leave them alone?"

"I didn't. What I mean is I brought Daddy back to my house. Mother was all but passed out, so I just covered her with some blankets and left notes for her every place I thought she might eventually focus her eyes telling her that Daddy is with me and to call me when she gets up."

"Not a very auspicious start to the New Year, is it?"

"No, but it really shouldn't be a surprise. We should just be grateful we got a couple of weeks' reprieve from the madness."

"What's your dad doing now?"

"He's staring at the TV screen. The last time I paid any attention, he was watching a program about some obscure bug that they thought was extinct but found again in the Amazon or something. Roger is lying beside him with his head in his lap. Looks like a Norman Rockwell painting, if you discount the fact that he doesn't understand a thing he's hearing and keeps saying 'nice kitty cat' while he rubs Roger's ears."

"Are you going to call Christine and the others?"

"Why? What could they do? It's pretty clear who's going to have to star in the role of warden in this flick."

Kate thought of pushing Casey to contact her siblings and then remembered her own experience with Martha and Jolene and knew that it was better left alone.

"How's the weather up there?"

"Lousy and getting worse. I think we'll end up iced in for at least a little while. Sure hope the power doesn't go out. I can find ways to keep warm, but Daddy needs the thermostat set just short of 'inferno' to keep from freezing. His circulation must be getting really bad. Times like this I really wish I had a fireplace."

"I wish I were there to be your personal space heater."

"That would be nice, Kate. I wish you were here, too, for that and about a dozen other reasons."

"I'm sorry—"

"Uh-oh. Daddy's on the prowl. I need to catch him before he gets out the front door, babe. Got to run."

"I love you, Casey. Happy New Year." The hollow hum of the dial tone was the only reply.

Chapter 24

Kate tried to call Casey's house half a dozen times before heading out for work the next morning. The news reports were telling of downed power lines and roads that looked like skating rinks all over the Carolinas, Tennessee, north Georgia, and parts of eastern Alabama.

"Well, she'll call as soon as she can," Kate consoled herself as she tried one last time from her cell phone before leaving the Volvo in her parking spot just up the street from the home office of DeWitt, Scroggins, and Howell. "Bernice can take the message and give it to me between clients." She pulled her briefcase out of the backseat and set the security alarm. It was cold and dank in downtown Atlanta, but at least the rain had stopped.

There was a steady parade in and out of Kate's office all day. As she ushered each set in and out, she hesitated ever so briefly on her way past her secretary's desk. "Any messages, Bernice?" she would ask. (As if Bernice had ever failed to deliver one.)

"No, sorry, Ms. Bingham," Bernice would reply. (As if she needed to be reminded to do something so simple.)

Tuesday raced by, thanks to her full schedule. She hated not being able to reach Casey, but in some ways, it was just as well since she wouldn't have had time to talk anyhow.

Tuesday night, Kate all but sat with her hand on the receiver, waiting for the phone to ring. It did once, about eight-thirty, and she dispatched that telemarketer with a swift, "I'm not interested. Take my number off your list."

Though she wasn't in the habit of surfing the local news offerings, she watched each network's recounting of the "surprise ice storm that was still paralyzing many parts of the viewing area," as each and every anchorman or woman said at least fifteen times in their half hour's allotment of time.

Wednesday morning was a carbon copy of Tuesday. Client after client after client and still no word from Delano, North Carolina. Kate had a twenty minute gap at lunchtime and used it to call Darren and Judy's house in Stockbridge and Margie and Ed's house in Alpharetta. Of course, everyone was at work, so all she could do was leave a message. "Hi, it's Kate Bingham. I haven't heard from Casey since Monday night. I know the ice storm has probably knocked out the lines, but if you should happen to get a call from her, would you call me, please, or have her call me?" She repeated her home, office, and cell numbers twice before hanging up.

Wednesday afternoon came and went, and still no call. The light on her answering machine was flashing when she got home, telling her she had two new messages. One was from Judy, Darren's wife, corroborating that they hadn't heard from Casey—nor from Nora, either. The other was Margie saying the same thing and encouraging Kate not to be concerned since phone service in the mountains of western North Carolina is an iffy proposition in an ice storm. Kate spent the remainder of Wednesday night waiting by the phone without so much as a call from someone trying to sell her vinyl siding or a subscription to a magazine She had almost rubbed the lettering off the redial button on the phone in the living room from trying Casey's house so many times.

The newspeople's line that night was "isolated pockets still without electricity or phone service, but crews are working to get everyone back on line." Casey didn't have a computer, so even if she did have electrical service, e-mail wasn't an option for trying to find her. Kate started toying with the notion of driving up to Delano, but from the sound of things, there were still lots of downed trees and roads that still weren't passable. Besides, tomorrow was another day of preliminary tax workups for long-standing patrons of DS & H. At midnight, she surrendered and flopped into bed for another fitful few hours of something approximating sleep.

On Thursday, just as she had the previous two mornings, Kate took the photo that Casey had given her as she was leaving Monday afternoon off her nightstand and dropped it into her briefcase with her package of yogurt-covered raisins and granola bar. She would have loved to put the picture of Casey and her adopted four-footers on her desk at the office, but that wouldn't have been in keeping with the professional persona of the heir apparent to the throne in New Haven. At least with it in her briefcase, she could steal a glance at it on those rare off-moments in her workday.

Early in the afternoon on Thursday, Bernice tapped softly on the door to Kate's office and let herself in. She stood just inside the doorway until Kate paused in her discussion of Alternative Minimum Tax with the couple sitting at the desk. Kate knew that Bernice was much too polished a professional to interrupt without good cause.

"Excuse me, just a moment, will you?" she said to the couple. Kate shifted her gaze to Bernice.

"Ms. Bingham, I am so sorry to bother you. May I see you in the outer office, please?"

Kate couldn't decipher the look on Bernice's face as she rose from behind her desk and preceded Bernice out the door.

"You've just had a call from Ms. Casey Marsden," Bernice began as she closed the door behind them. "I remembered her as one of

Nora's daughters from all those years that Nora worked in this office. I offered to put her through to you, but she said she only had a minute and asked if I would please give you a message."

Kate was still stymied in trying to read Bernice's countenance.

"OK . . ." Kate drew out the second syllable to prompt Bernice to get on with the message relay.

"She said to tell you that there has been a terrible accident and that she needs you to come right away."

Kate blanched and felt her knees buckle. "Oh, no. Dear God, no." Kate took a couple of deep breaths. "Did she say who's hurt, Bernice? What else did she tell you?"

"Really, Ms. Bingham, that's about all. She did say not to bother calling the house because she wasn't there, but she didn't tell me where you might find her instead."

Kate's mind reeled. Was Casey hurt? Had something happened to Burr? To Nora? To both of them? To all of them? She had to go!

"Damn. I'm right in the middle of the worksheet with these people." Kate gestured toward the door to her office.

"I took the liberty of asking Ms. Collins to finish this interview for you. Her one o'clock canceled and she's free for the rest of the afternoon. She can take your other two clients as well."

"Bernice, you're one in a million. Thank you." Kate feared she might start crying right there in the open area of the outer office.

"It's all part of my job, Ms. Bingham." Bernice fleetingly looked away, then met Kate's gaze again. "I know that you and Nora Marsden were very good friends when both you and she worked here a number of years ago. When I spoke to her a few months back, she told me that you had been to see her and her husband several times since you came back to Atlanta. I always thought very highly of Nora. If there is something that I can help with, I hope you'll let me know."

Even in her state of mental chaos, Kate had a flash of insight. Nora Marsden and Bernice Easton had kept in touch beyond Nora's retirement. When Kate rejoined the Atlanta office, she and Bernice had rekindled their association, albeit a somewhat arms'-length one moreso than one of personal friendship. She had provided Bernice with a sketchy update of her life over the intervening years, including the death of her father following an extended stay at a nursing home. Kate surmised that Bernice was the one who had told Nora about Ray Bingham's final circumstances. At least one mystery was solved.

Now she needed to focus on the current mystery of what was going on a hundred miles up the road in Delano.

"Do you need anything besides your coat, Ms. Bingham?" Bernice asked. "It might be easier if I make your apologies and collect your things from inside." She inclined her head toward the door of Kate's office.

"My briefcase, in the bottom drawer of the credenza behind my desk. My keys and everything else are in there."

Bernice was in and back out in a minute's time.

"Call me when you can, OK?" Bernice reminded Kate as she handed her the coat and briefcase. Kate headed for the bank of elevators. "And don't worry about this place," Bernice assured her. "I'll keep tabs on things for you."

Kate raced home, yanked her suit and pantyhose off, and fumbled into jeans and a shirt and sweater. She swept an armload of toiletries into the tote bag still beside the dresser where it had landed Monday evening. She crammed some undergarments and an oddball assortment of turtlenecks, slacks, shoes, sweatclothes, and socks in with them and sprinted back to the elevator that took her down to her car in the parking ramp below her condominium building.

She stopped for gas at exit four on Interstate 985 halfway to Gainesville. Blessedly, the temperatures had moderated to well above freezing, so all vestiges of the surprise ice storm had vanished and she had clear roads for the drive. She was making good time, but the miles seemed to drag by in slow motion. She thought of trying to find Darren or Margie via her cell phone, but then decided that, since she had no idea what had happened, there would be little point in doing so.

Finally she saw the familiar billboards that told her she was near Delano. She swung off Highway 441 onto Highway 64 and then began the series of turns that would take her to Casey's house. Then she remembered that Casey had told Bernice to tell her she wouldn't be at the house. Kate changed course and headed for Nora's house instead.

Kate hadn't realized how lost in thought she was until she almost missed the turn into Burr and Nora's subdivision. She rounded the corner and had to stomp the brakes and steer sharply to her right to avoid a sleek black hearse that was just about to turn left from the one-lane paved street of the subdivision out onto the main roadway.

"Please, God. Please don't let that be Burr," Kate prayed.

Kate made the final turns and pulled into the Marsden's yard. The Volvo skidded to a halt on the gravel driveway. Casey's truck was there, as were both of her parents' vehicles, so at least it hadn't been a car wreck that constituted the "terrible accident" that Bernice mentioned as part of Casey's cryptic message. Kate ripped the key from the ignition and tore to the front door. She turned the knob and it gave way beneath her hand.

Burr was sitting on the sofa in the living room. No one else was anywhere in sight.

Burr looked up as Kate burst through the door. He seemed to recognize her and felt compelled to offer an explanation.

"You'll have to excuse me if I don't seem myself tonight." He started to weep softly. "You see, I just found out that my mother died today."

Chapter 25

"His mother?" Kate asked as Casey appeared from the bathroom just up the hall from the living room. "I was sure you'd told me that all your grandparents are dead."

"He's a little confused," Casey explained as she drew Kate off to the kitchen doorway. "It's Mother—my mother."

Kate, weary from her drive and from three nights of precious little sleep and from incessant worry, looked at Casey, transfixed and uncomprehending.

"She's dead, Kate. My mother is dead."

"Oh Casey! I'm so sorry. How? When? What happened?"

"I don't want to say too much about it, if you know what I mean." Casey swung her head to look at her father, still sitting on the sofa, tears trickling down his cheeks. Kate nodded to express her understanding.

"I'm glad you're here." Casey enveloped Kate in her arms. She shuddered and exhaled in stutter steps.

"I got here as fast as I could," Kate assured her as they disengaged from one another's arms.

"I know you've just spent two hours on the road, but do you think you could run over to my house and see about Roger and the cats? I've been over here since before noon, and I'm pretty sure I left without putting any food and water down for them."

"Sure, Casey."

"I'm going to try to get him to eat some supper and then I'll coax him to bed early. I've got something to help him relax, so I'm hoping he'll drop off without much of a fight." Kate had to strain to hear Casey's words. "After you've been to my place, come on back here. We can talk then."

Kate regarded Casey carefully. There was no color in her cheeks and her face was drawn. Her shining blue eyes, always her best feature, were flat and lifeless. Certainly she was entitled to be distressed, probably to the point of nearly being in shock, but Kate sensed something more than grief and devastating emotional trauma.

"I'm really sorry about your mom, babe."

"Not half as sorry as I am." There was a caustic undertone to Casey's words.

"Do we have any cornbread, honey? I'm hungry." Burr looked plaintively toward his daughter and her companion.

"I'll make us some, Daddy. Why don't you come sit here in the kitchen while I fix us a bite to eat?" She took a few steps toward Burr to help guide him to a chair by the small table in the corner of the kitchen.

Kate took that as her cue to leave.

"I'll be back as quickly as I can. Do you need me to bring you anything from your house?"

"No. Darren is supposed to head up here right after work. As soon as he gets here, we can go back to our house to sleep."

With a wave of her hand, Kate was out the door and on her way to Casey's place. Three animals that acted as though they hadn't eaten in a week instead of only twelve hours greeted her at the door in eager anticipation. Roger, of course, first needed the immediate respite of flying out the door to keep his bladder from disintegrating, but he was back in record time, reminding Kate that the dry dog food was kept in a can with a secure lid on a shelf above the dryer. To salve her conscience, she opened canned food for all of them and made sure the portions were a little more generous than usual.

Once the food bowls were on the floor, Kate took advantage of the time they were eating to survey the rest of the house. There was no mistaking that Burr had spent much of the preceding couple of days there. While no one would ever accuse Casey of being a fastidious housekeeper, she was not in the habit of having her father's socks draped over the arm of the sofa or his underwear on the corner of the entertainment center or of storing a can of shaving foam on the kitchen sink. The double bed in the second bedroom looked as though it had been used as a testing ground for the durability of fitted sheets. There were wrappers from packets of cheese and crackers lying on the small chest of drawers, on the nightstand, and under the foot of the bed. The hall bath had used towels flung everywhere from the floor to the doorknob, as well as a pile of Burr's pants and shirts in the corner by the tub. The shower curtain was hanging from only nine of its dozen rings. Casey's bedroom looked better than the rest of the house, although there were uncharacteristic heaps of dirty clothes stacked on the rocking chair and on the far side of the bed, and the vanity in the adjoining bath was in need of a wipe-down.

"Burr Marsden, interior desecrator," Kate observed to herself. "Casey sure didn't get her flair for home beautification from her paternal genes."

Her reconnoiter complete, Kate set about making sure that the water bowls were cleaned and refilled and that the bowl of dry kibble for the kitties was replenished. Roger had licked every morsel from his bowl, leaving it clean as the proverbial hound's tooth and was happy for the chance to go back outside to determine if aliens of any

143

sort had passed through his yard. Kate cleaned and refilled the litter boxes and picked up the saucers from which Kit and Caboodle had just feasted and placed them in the dishwasher.

She made a quick sweep through the entire house with a large plastic trash bag in hand gathering up Burr's possessions. She deposited the bag by the front door and then did a slapdash cleaning of both bathrooms. On her final pass, she dragged the laundry basket from room to room, loading towels, the sheets from the second bedroom, and Casey's dirty clothes into it as she went. She set the basket on the washing machine and then summoned a reluctant Roger to the door.

"Your mama and I should be back in just a couple of hours, Buddy," Kate consoled him as she dried his feet. "Sorry you've had such a lonely day." Roger pitched himself over at a sharp angle so that all of his weight was resting on Kate's legs. "I know. You're a poor, neglected darling who just wants someone home all day every day to scratch his belly." Roger flopped to the floor, rolled to his back, and turned his round underside up so that Kate could make good on her observation.

"You little clown. Now you're going to try to convince me that you understood what I just said. Nothing but happenstance, sir." Roger didn't care. He grunted and groaned appreciatively as Kate massaged his bulging tummy.

Kate stepped back into the kitchen from the utility room, lifted the phone from the wall, and punched in Burr and Nora's number.

"Hi. I'm about ready to head back over there. Have you thought of anything you need?"

"Just you, Kate."

"See you in a little bit."

The clock in the dashboard registered six forty-five. Kate hadn't eaten since noon, and that was only raisins and granola bars. She grabbed her cell phone and called Casey as she turned the key in the ignition.

"Hi. Me again. I know you're going to tell me you don't feel like eating, but I was thinking I might swing by Many Fortunes and pick up something."

"You're right, I don't feel much like eating, but I could probably eat a little foo young or something like that. Nothing spicy, though."

"Got it. Give me an extra ten minutes to do that. I'll be there by seven fifteen."

With her penchant for numbers, Kate only needed to use a phone number once to have it permanently locked in her memory. She placed the call to Many Fortunes for a carry-out order of vegetable foo young and chicken lo mein.

"That was quick." Casey met Kate at the door with a kiss and outstretched hands to take the brown sack Kate was clutching to her chest with one hand while she carried the trash bag full of Burr's things from Casey's house with the other.

"Not much of a crowd at Many Fortunes on a Thursday night," Kate explained.

"What's that?" Casey pointed to the trash bag.

"Anything I found at your house that looked like it belongs to your dad." Kate let it fall to the floor and nudged it aside with her foot. "How's he doing?"

"Sound asleep, thank God." Casey had taken the carry-out bag to the counter and was standing there with her back to Kate. Kate moved near her and placed a hand on her shoulder to turn her so that they were facing one another.

"What about you? How are you doing?"

Casey dissolved. "It's all my fault, Kate," she howled. "I can't believe I let this happen." Casey shook so hard it was all Kate could do to keep her on her feet.

"Stop, Casey. Stop." She took Casey firmly by her upper arms. "Come sit down with me and tell me what happened."

They found their way to the tea rose chintz loveseat. As they sat, Kate couldn't help but wish that they were in Casey's house instead of Nora's. The atmosphere at Casey's was homey and inviting; here she felt stultified and confined.

"Catch your breath, and then start at the beginning and tell me everything."

It took Casey a few moments to get her breathing back under control. She wiped her eyes on her sleeve and began.

"You know that I came over here Monday afternoon after you'd left to go back to Atlanta. Mother was drunk. Daddy had hauled food everywhere—the place looked like hell.

"I figured she'd just sleep it off, so I grabbed pajamas and some clothes and stuff for Daddy and took him back to my place, thinking that I'd bring him back the next morning. I took a couple of changes of clothes because he always spills on himself when he eats and he doesn't always get to the bathroom in time. Well, anyway, like I just said, I only thought I'd have him overnight, but then the ice storm hit.

"The power flickered on and off five or six times that evening, but it always came back on, so I thought we were going to be OK, but sometime during the night, it went off and stayed off. When I got up Tuesday morning, it already was starting to feel like a meat locker in the house. I tried to call Mother—you, too, of course—but the phone was dead. That had happened last year when we got ice, so it wasn't like it spooked me or anything.

"Can you imagine trying to keep Daddy entertained without television to serve as his electronic babysitter? I was ready to join a convent by noon the first day. We didn't get power back till afternoon on Wednesday. Geez, was that just yesterday? But the phone still wasn't working. I was really worried about Mother being here all by herself. I figured her power was out too, so I worried that she'd try to start a fire in the fireplace downstairs and forget to open the flue and asphyxiate herself. Or worse, I was afraid that she'd get a roaring fire going and then have too much booze or too many pills and burn the place down. Of course I couldn't call her, so there was no way to know what was going on here.

"At least with the power back on, I had a better chance of keeping Daddy occupied. All of the news reports said that trees were still blocking lots of roads, especially private ones, and that only the major roads had been treated with sand and salt. I probably could have inched the moo mobile down off my hill, but I was pretty sure I'd never make it the eleven miles to get over here. Last year, the roads in this subdivision were impassable for almost a week after a two-day freezing rain. If it were just me, I could have driven as far as I could get and then hiked the rest of the way, but what would I do with Daddy? I couldn't leave him at my place alone and I couldn't risk having to leave him in my truck by himself somewhere along the road. And for sure, he wouldn't have been able to walk even a quarter of a mile with me, so I was pretty much trapped.

"Finally by late this morning it had warmed up enough that we could drive over here. I was so exhausted from keeping up with him I almost didn't have the strength to push the clutch in.

"It was still pretty foggy and overcast when we pulled in. The cars were both sitting where they always do, so I took that as a good sign. There were lots of lights on in the house, so I thought Mother was up and functioning. I took that as a good sign, too. I figured we'd have a little fight and call each other some names and that would be that.

"When we came through the door, I knew right away something was wrong. It felt funny, smelled funny, sounded funny. I started calling for Mother, but my voice just echoed off the walls. Daddy started calling out, too, yelling 'Mother, Mother.' He had never called her that ever before, but I guess he knew we were looking for someone and wanted to be part of the search.

"First place I looked was in the sewing room because that's where I'd left her on New Year's Day. I thought maybe she had overdosed or had a heart attack or a stroke or something, but she wasn't there. The bed was all messed up, but it had been that way before I left.

"I checked her bedroom. The bed was still made with all the throw pillows still in their perfect little row. The drawer on her nightstand was open, but otherwise, it didn't look like anything else was any different than usual.

"I looked in the guest room and all the bathrooms. Nothing out of the ordinary in the least. Daddy, of course, was with me step for step, still calling out every few seconds.

"The only place left to look was the basement. I came back down the hallway and flipped the switch for the stairwell, and that's when I saw her." For the first time since starting the reiteration, Casey's eyes welled and her voice failed her. Kate waited silently, her open hand resting on Casey's upper leg.

"It was just awful, Kate. She was all twisted and crumpled down on the lower landing. Her neck and head were at this impossible angle to the rest of her body and I knew right away she was dead."

Again Kate waited while the heartsick woman beside her fought for equanimity.

"I raced down the stairs, even though I knew it was too late. As I got close to her, I could see that her lips and fingernails were blue. She was just as cold and stiff as—" The memory was more than Casey could tolerate.

"That's so sad, Casey. I'm sorry you had to be the one to find her."

"The coroner told me before he left that her neck was broken in two places. He said it was over before she even knew what happened." She sniffed aloud. "I think he just said that to try to make me feel better. Like maybe if I thought that she didn't suffer it wouldn't matter so much that she was dead."

"It's better than thinking she lay there for a day or more in pain, isn't it?"

"Oh, I don't know," Casey shot back in frustration. "No matter what, it's still my fault, Kate. I never should have left her here by herself. I knew she was drunk. I should have taken her home with me. Or I should have stayed here or something. It's my fault she's dead." The flash of remorse in Casey's eyes ricocheted around the room.

"Sweetheart, you couldn't have known this would happen. It was an accident. There's probably no way to tell for certain when she fell or if she was drunk or on pills when she did. She lost her footing and fell down that long run of stairs. You did what you thought was the right thing to do when you took your dad home with you. The whole situation took an unexpected turn—one that had the worst possible outcome—but don't punish yourself for something you didn't do."

"While I was waiting for the emergency people to get here, I looked in the medicine cabinet to see if I could tell if she'd been taking any of her drugs."

"What did you find?"

"The antacid bottle was where she had the sleeping pills. She had a note in with them that said so. There must have been twenty-five of them when I looked on Monday."

"Today—?"

"Only three. And then I checked the other bottles and boxes. There weren't but one or two pills in any of them and there were lots more than that just a couple of days ago."

"So what are you saying, Casey?"

"What if she took them all on purpose?"

"You mean intentionally overdosed?"

"Just say it outright, Kate! Maybe she tried to kill herself."

"Oh, Casey, why would she do that?" Kate was appalled at the notion and made no attempt to hide it.

"Because I took Daddy out of here and she thought I was going to lock him up in some loony bin somewhere and because that would mean that she was a failure and that everyone would know it."

"Listen to me." Kate took Casey's face between her palms. "You can spend from now till eternity trying to play out every possible scenario for what went on here over the past seventy-two hours. For all we know, your mom realized that she'd made a mistake in getting her prescriptions refilled and flushed them down the commode. We won't ever, ever know, Casey. Even if you had been here and she was stone cold sober and straight, she might have tripped and fallen down the steps."

Casey let the possibility of what Kate suggested and the relief of the potential reprieve from responsibility roll around in her head for a while.

"Want to know the saddest part?" Casey didn't wait for Kate's answer. "Right beside her on the landing was the little flashlight from her nightstand—the one that she took the batteries out of so that she could bury her pills in it instead. My guess is that the power went out here sometime that first night just like it did at my house and she went to get that flashlight to help her find her way around. Fat lot of good it did her," Casey concluded ruefully.

"What happened after you found her?"

"Daddy followed me down to the landing. He was still yelling for 'mother,' whoever he thought that might be. He looked at his wife of forty-some years dead at his feet and said, as only my father in his current state can say, 'Are we going to have lunch soon?' "

"Oh, Casey, he didn't know what was going on . . ."

"No, he didn't, he doesn't, and he never will again." Casey pursed her lips and sighed from deep within herself. "I brought him back upstairs with me and parked him in front of the television. Then I called nine-one-one. I made a quick call to your office and then found Margie at work and told her to call the others. I spent the rest of the day dealing with the coroner, the medical examiner, the sheriff, the funeral home—and, of course, my father, who eventually picked up on enough of what was swirling around him to start telling everyone who'd listen that his mother had just died."

Casey cocked her head back and stared at the ceiling. "Now that I stop to think about it, that's exactly what did happen. She's been much more his mother than his wife for months and months." With an effort, Casey got to her feet and flexed her neck and shoulders.

"And I guess I'll be the next person starring in that role."

Chapter 26

Darren and Judy and their two children got to Burr's house just before ten o'clock Thursday night. Casey gave the adults a cursory recounting of what had happened to augment the very limited information she had given Darren earlier on the phone. She answered most of their questions with "I'll tell you the rest of it tomorrow."

Casey left her sleeping father in her brother's care and gladly acquiesced when Kate offered to drive the two of them back to her house. Neither of them slept well, and by dawn, they both were up making preparations for the day.

Kate and Casey were back at Burr's by eight the next morning. Judy had fixed breakfast for everyone, but no one other than Burr and his grandchildren had much of an appetite. Margie and Ed and their son arrived just after noon. Kate volunteered to stay with Burr and the three youngsters while Casey and her two siblings and their spouses went to the funeral home to begin making arrangements for

Nora's services. Christine wasn't expected from Florida until the next day and had told them to go ahead without her. Despite several calls to San Francisco, no one had as yet managed to speak ear-to-ear with BJ. Given the time difference and the odd hours he kept, it was anyone's guess when he'd get their messages and call back to North Carolina to get the full story of his mother's death.

When he did call, Kate was still holding down the fort at the Marsden residence. She relayed much of what Casey had told her the night before, leaving out the more gruesome of the details in deference to the grandchildren being within earshot.

Kate told him that she was sure the family would arrange for his airfare. He only hesitated a moment before he told her that he wouldn't be coming for the funeral.

"I just saw her two weeks ago. She was alive and beautiful and that's how I want to remember her," BJ said plainly. "I'm not interested in seeing her lying in a box looking like a plastic replica of herself with her hair and makeup done all wrong." Kate could tell there would be no dissuading him from his decision.

"I'll tell Casey and the others," Kate said simply. "They'll miss you."

"Some of them might. Some of them won't." He didn't sound bitter, just matter-of-fact.

"I'm sorry about your mother, BJ." Kate waited for a response but BJ didn't offer one. "And I'm sorry I didn't get to spend more time with you at Christmas. Maybe when you're here next time . . ."

"If there is a next time. With Mother gone, I'm not sure there'd be much point."

A long, awkward silence followed.

"Well, thanks for the information, Kate. I hope the funeral goes OK. Bye."

"Good-bye, BJ." Just before she put the phone back on the cradle she heard him speak again. She drew the receiver back to her ear.

"Oh, and, Kate, be good to my kid sister. I could tell she's crazy about you. I hope that whole thing works out."

The line went dead before Kate could react.

With others available to keep Burr out of harm's way and to make a couple of trips to Casey's house to tend her animals, on Saturday, Kate and Casey drove back to Atlanta so that Kate could pick up appropriate clothing to wear to the viewing Sunday night and the funeral Monday afternoon. Rather than push themselves to get back to Delano, they spent the night at Kate's condo—the first time they had ever done so.

Too tired for conversation or much else, they crashed into bed early and each had the first decent night's sleep they'd enjoyed in what felt like weeks. Before leaving Atlanta Sunday morning to head back up the road, they went by Kate's office. She left a detailed note on Bernice's desk outlining the specifics for Nora's services Monday. It wasn't likely that anyone from DeWitt, Scroggins, and Howell could rearrange their schedules to be there, but Kate had only found time for one very brief call to Bernice on Friday afternoon to give her the barest of information about Nora's death. She knew that Nora still had friends in the office and that they would want to know the plans, even if they couldn't attend.

The viewing at the funeral home was scheduled from six-thirty to eight-thirty Sunday evening. The children had tried to prepare their father for what was expected of him, but they might as well have tried to nail gelatin to the wall. By the end of the first half hour, Casey had extracted Burr from the situation that was confusing him beyond all measure and taken him back to his house.

After the Sunday evening debacle at the funeral home, Casey and her brother and sisters debated not taking Burr to the funeral on Monday but finally decided that they had to at least try to have him there.

Monday afternoon was brisk but bearable and sunny, about the best one can hope for in early January in the Smokies. Kate's heart warmed when she saw Bernice Easton step into the First Baptist Church of Delano. Kate was standing in the narthex, apart from Burr and the Marsden children as they greeted people entering, but on standby to take Burr to another part of the church if the need arose. If Bernice was surprised to see Kate Bingham sitting with the immediate family during the service, she had the good grace to keep it to herself.

Burr made it halfway through the service, but when he started singing bits and snatches of every hymn he had ever heard in a voice so loud that the minister could barely be heard, Kate led him out of the pew and down the side aisle out of the sanctuary. She took him to the fellowship hall in the basement where she entertained him with snacks of finger foods from the serving platters that would be offered to the mourners following the graveside ceremony. Several times he asked why they were there and wondered when they could go back home. He occasionally reiterated his lament that his mother had died, but that, too, seemed to be a rapidly fading memory.

In hindsight, all of Nora's children would remark that the entire time surrounding her death and funeral service was lost in a time warp where the days both sped by in a heartbeat and dragged on interminably. In years to come, when they would speak of those days in early January, they would find that each recalled something very different from what the others remembered in regards to all but one detail—there simply was no lingering doubt that Burr needed to be placed in a facility where he could get full-time care.

The siblings (minus BJ in California, who made it clear that he was more than content to be left out of the discussions) contemplated looking for a home somewhere in Atlanta so that Burr would be nearer to two of his children, but when push came to shove at screening the available resources, no one felt they had the time (or desire) to comb through the options. By default, the Morning Sun Assisted Living Quarters near Asheville won their approval as the location where Burleson Marsden would live out the next part of his life.

Since Casey had already made preliminary arrangements for Burr to be admitted there, it fell to her to move them along from tentative to definite. The simplest route was to have Casey named as Burr's legal guardian with Darren as her backup. There were some legal hoops to jump through to get the paperwork put in place, and, of course, the arduous process of sorting through everything in the house still loomed before them. Nora's things and Burr's possessions all had to be dealt with. For once, the four youngest Marsden children were able to keep their sights on a common goal and work for the common good.

They didn't want to rush Burr out of the house. After all, he had just buried his wife, even if he wasn't exactly sure what that term should mean to him. Darren's wife, Judy, and the three sisters—Christine, Margie, and Casey—composed a workable schedule for the four of them to split and share the tasks involved in getting the house cleaned out and keeping Burr out from under foot while that was underway.

Morning Sun would admit Burr on February first, or hold the room for him for up to two months (with full payment, of course, whether he was there or not) if the family needed more time to make the transition. The Marsdens knew that they couldn't begin to have the house emptied that quickly, but perhaps by late spring when the real estate market was likely to have its usual burst of activity, they could have the house ready to be put up for sale.

Kate stayed in Delano through the Tuesday immediately following the funeral. That made a total of three and a half days of work that she had missed. As she had noted to Casey on New Year's Day, getting even one day behind this early in the busy season was a sure route to heartburn.

Kate hated to admit it even to herself, but she was jealous at how Casey and her sisters and sister-in-law had united to tackle the onerous undertakings confronting the family following Nora's sudden death and the unavoidable conclusion regarding Burr's need for professional nursing attention. It made the contentious, unsupportive experience that she had had with her own sisters when dealing with her father's comparable need some six years earlier all the more acrid to recall. But given the mountain of backlogged work that assaulted her when she returned to her desk at DS & H, she had hardly more than one free minute to consider the comparison.

Kate was so swamped that she stayed in Atlanta and worked two ten-hour days the first weekend following Nora's funeral. It was just as well, because Casey was just as overwhelmed up in Delano. Christine was still there and Margie returned for the weekend, so there wouldn't have been any time for Kate and Casey to spend together anyway.

They did manage to squeeze in time for a pithy phone call to one another every night, but they both were so brain-dead that "I love you; I miss you; I'll talk to you tomorrow," was about sum and substance of each exchange.

The second weekend following the funeral, Kate took a time-out from her accounting responsibilities and traced the familiar route to Casey's house.

"I didn't realize till this very second just how much I missed you." Kate was barely inside the door to Casey's great room. They were kissing and touching and kissing some more.

"Me too, babe." Casey reluctantly released Kate from her arms. "And the furry family members have missed you as well." Roger was nearly as enthusiastic as Casey in his greeting of Kate. Kit and Caboodle had even managed to bestir themselves from the bedroom to wend and weave around Kate's ankles.

Casey took Kate by the hand and piloted her to the sofa. "We've got about two hours. Margie and Ed are with Daddy. Darren is supposed to be up here around noon. I said I'd be over there by twelve or twelve-thirty." They all but sat in one another's laps as they dropped onto the sofa. "Tell me everything," Casey commanded.

"Work, work, work, and then for variety, work. That catches you up on my life." Kate caressed the side of Casey's face. "You look tired. Are you getting any sleep?"

"Some. Enough. It's hard because there's so much to do. Most week nights, I end up bringing Daddy here. I always feel like I have to keep one ear open all night, if you know what I mean."

"Yeah, I think I do." Kate slid her hand to the far side of Casey's face and lifted her head so that she could kiss her lips.

"We really shouldn't, Kate. I mean we're supposed to be over at the house in just a little while—" Casey's protest was weak, and Kate knew it.

"We're both too pooped to do much." She stood and Casey joined her.

Back in the bedroom, fully clothed, they stretched out full length face to face.

"If we fall asleep, we'll be the living representation of that old Everly Brothers song," Casey joked.

"Don't worry, Little Susie," Kate rejoined, "I have no intention of letting you sleep."

And she didn't.

Chapter 27

"I can't believe you'd even think of asking me that, Kate!" Casey was slamming cans, food bowls, and silverware on the counter in the kitchen with such force that the animals had scurried from the room without getting breakfast.

"All I said was since it looks like you guys will be ready to move your dad into Morning Sun in another couple of weeks, maybe we could talk about New Haven again."

"You just don't get it, do you Kate?"

"Apparently not." She waited for her own temper to cool and then continued. "Why don't you explain it to me again?"

"I'm not going to New Haven."

"But why not, Casey? I thought the entire issue was that you couldn't leave your parents. That whole thing is the same as resolved. I'm sorry as I can be that your mom died and I hate that your dad is in the throes of dementia, but at least you know that he'll be well cared for at Morning Sun." Kate could feel her voice rising, so she stopped to calm herself. "I just don't see what's holding you here."

"I like it here," Casey snarled through clenched teeth. "No, correction. I *love* it here. I consider this house and these mountains my home. I told you that the first time we talked about this, but you seem to have conveniently forgotten it."

"No, I didn't forget. If you'd care to remember, I told you that New Haven wouldn't be for all time and eternity. It's just a stepping stone. I fully expect to be back in Atlanta in two years or less." She softened her tone and appended, "I thought that we could make a new home together."

"As if being back in Atlanta would solve anything, Kate!" Casey exploded. "I don't want to live in Atlanta any more than I want to live in New Haven." Casey held out her left hand, cupped. "Cities. Noise, traffic, crowds, pollution, aggravations." She lifted her right hand and cupped it to match her left. "Country living. Quiet, privacy, open roads, clean air, peace." She moved her hands up and down as though balancing a scale. "Let's see, which is better . . ."

"We could keep your place here, Casey. Rent it out while we're in New Haven and then use it ourselves as a weekend place once we're back in Atlanta."

"Yeah, Roger and the cats can go a week at a time without food or potty breaks or having their boxes cleaned. That's assuming, of course, they figure out how to survive while we go chase the almighty dollar for two years in Connecticut."

"They'd adjust to the move, Casey. We could get a house with a yard up there instead of the condo on the beach like we talked about."

"Like *you* talked about, Kate! I don't care if it's an oceanfront condo or a house in the suburbs or a mansion surrounded by a ten-foot brick wall. I don't want to move to New Haven or anywhere else for that matter. I'm home." Casey looked around the room as if to verify her comment. "But obviously, you're not, so if you need to go, you need to go."

"But Casey—"

"But nothing. Even if you want to disregard everything I've just said, remember this: my father will be in a nursing home just up the road from here. I am the one most likely to go see him and most likely to be the one who decides what's best for him from here on out. I am not about to up and leave him." Casey's voice wavered but she choked the words out anyway. "I've just lost one parent—probably because I failed to pay enough attention to her. I'll be damned if I'm going to voluntarily surrender the only one I've got left. I know I can't keep him at home like Mother would have wanted me to. That's all the more reason not to run out on him. And for what? Just so that you can make an even bigger stack of money every year and get a new title behind your name?"

"Maybe we'd better not talk about this any more right now," Kate said evenly.

"And maybe my mother was right. Maybe you don't understand that in this family, we take care of our own."

Kate's eyes flashed fire. She looked toward Casey and opened her mouth to speak, but she knew that angry words would only make a bad situation worse. She swallowed hard and waited a moment before offering a deflective comment. "I think I'll go watch TV in the bedroom for a while."

"I think it might be better if you got your crap and went back to Atlanta." Casey stood with her hands on her hips, her jaw jutting toward Kate. "Take your expensive imported car and go back to your skyline view ritzy apartment—oh, excuse me, I mean 'condo,' " she corrected, sarcastically "and your custom-made suits and silk blouses and special rugs and your 'it's an original, you know' artwork."

Kate started to walk away toward the hallway to the bedroom.

"Like anybody gives a flipping fig, Kate." Casey lobbed her final salvo.

"Like anybody gives a flipping fig," Kate mimicked, but had the good sense to keep walking.

Once in the bedroom, Kate began pulling her things from the

drawers and closet shelves where she had been accumulating her possessions, little by little, over the past four months. She jammed what she could into her canvas tote bag, but there was still a sizable pile heaped on the bed. Then she remembered that she'd brought a small carry-on bag with her the day she and Casey had driven to Atlanta to pick up clothes for her to wear for Nora's funeral. She'd left it behind when she'd gone back to the city. She got it out of the closet and shoved the remainder of her belongings in and zipped the lid.

As Kate returned to the great room, Casey was standing by the small table near the front door. "I think I got everything," Kate indicated, trying to keep all emotion out of her voice. She hoped Casey would offer an apology or an olive branch, but she didn't.

"OK. Good."

"So this is it, Casey?" Kate searched Casey's face for some clue.

"If you ever decide to accept me for what I am instead of trying to make me into some kind of Nikki Irving clone, look me up. I'll most likely be right here."

Kate felt the bile rising in her throat. Through sheer force of will, she held her tongue. She shifted the tote bag so that it sat atop the wheeled carry-on suitcase, freeing a hand so that she could open the front door. The feeble warmth of the late January sun fell across her face.

Kate stepped out of Casey Marsden's house and, she feared, out of Casey Marsden's life forever.

Chapter 28

Try as she might, Kate Bingham could not remember ever feeling more devastated. She was twenty-one when her mother died a quarter century ago. No, they hadn't been close, but she could still summon up the sense of desertion that had ensued following her funeral. Her mother was forty-seven when the pancreatic cancer snatched her away. Kate would be forty-seven on her next birthday. What if this were all the life that she (Kate) were to be given? Would it be enough? No, it most assuredly would not. Kate had a long list of things she still wanted to do before she died.

Her father's death was a more haunting loss. Even now, she ached for his sense of humor, for the way that she always felt safe when she was with him. When he was in the nursing home and lost within the mazes in his mind, she had to act like the parent to his helpless child, but she never fully surrendered the belief that he would always be her protector and provider. When he died, she was an orphan, albeit a forty-year-old one. But she could resurrect the sense of comfort she had following that loss knowing that she was going home to Nikki.

Nikki Irving. That hurt still ravaged her. Why had Casey hurled that horrible accusation at her as she was leaving? What did Casey Marsden know about her relationship with Nikki anyway? Kate had never treated Nikki badly. And even if she had—which she hadn't, dammit—she had never been unkind to Casey.

The maelstrom of reflections and recriminations swirled and crashed in Kate's mind until she was on the verge of screaming out loud. She checked the quartz clock on her desk in the corner of the living room. Two a.m. It had been nearly eighteen hours since Casey had thrown her out. In another four hours, she'd need to shower and get ready for work. She had been pacing the floor for so long that her arches ached from the exertion. She had opened and closed the vertical blinds to the balcony at least fifty times. She was hungry, but she couldn't eat. She was tired, but she couldn't sleep. She was sad— miserably sad, but much, much too sad for anything so simple as crying.

For the hundredth time, she asked herself and any gods who might be listening, "Why is Casey being so stubborn about going to New Haven? And why did she accuse me of trying to make her into another Nikki Irving?" Kate leaned against the sliding glass door to the balcony and looked at the artificial stars in the Atlanta night. "All I want is for her to go with me and to enjoy the things I could buy for us. Is that so wrong?"

The cold night air had cooled the glass and suddenly Kate was shivering with a chill that felt like it came from her deepest core. She trembled down the short hallway to her bedroom and saw the tote bag still on the bed where it had landed when she got home. She dumped it out to search for a sweatshirt to slip into.

"Oh, crap. That's Casey's." Kate pulled an oversized navy blue sweatshirt out of the jumble that the tote bag had disgorged. It was the same one that Casey had loaned her the day she had gone to Delano at Casey's request to spend an unannounced afternoon with

Nora and Burr—the day she had first seen why Casey was so concerned for both of her parents' mental states. Somehow, it had gotten mixed in with Kate's things. Without thinking, she lifted the sweatshirt to her face and inhaled deeply, just in case.

It was both wonderful and heartrending. It still smelled just like Casey—that mix of fresh, clean earth and the musk perfume that always made Kate want to start shedding her clothes every time she encountered it, especially in the curve of Casey's neck.

"Oh, Casey." It was somewhere between a prayer and a curse.

Kate noticed something else in the mix of things on her bed. It was the framed photo of Casey, Roger, Caboodle, and Kit. She picked it up by the hinged arm on the back of the frame. That made the backing slide out of the wooden frame, letting the picture and the matting fall free. When Kate plucked it from the coverlet, she discovered that there was a second, smaller picture taped to the reverse of the one she had so lovingly carried with her for the past several weeks.

It was a reduced copy of the grouping of Casey and the pets. Glued to it was another tiny cut-out photo. Even in the dim light of the bedroom, Kate could see that it was a picture of her, probably lifted from another shot that had been on the same roll that Christine had taken while everyone was at Burr and Nora's on Christmas day and then finished shooting at Casey's. Then she noticed that there was a handwritten note across the bottom of the collage. "All that's missing is you. We love you. Casey and the kids."

At long last the tears that Kate had been denied since leaving Delano sprang from her eyes. She pulled the navy blue sweatshirt over her head and hugged the photo to her chest. With the tears came the clarity that she so longed for.

She walked back to the main room of the apartment. "Yes, apartment, you fool, not condominium," she chided aloud. She looked around at all the trappings of her success: the Indian dhurrie under the dining table, the Turkish kilim beneath the chrome-and-glass coffee table in front of the divan, the artist's proofs and numbered prints hanging on the walls. "They're rugs and pictures and it's a sofa, for heaven's sake." Kate was actually smiling through her tears. The kitchen was next. Noritake china, Cuisinart food processor, Williams-Sonoma carafe, Calphalon cookware. "Dishes, blender, pitcher, pots and pans." Kate had the hang of it now.

She went back to the bedroom and opened the doors to the walk-in closet—a space large enough to qualify as a dwelling for a family of four in many Asian countries. She began counting the suits—many of them custom-made—hanging in her closet. She had tallied the gray ones, the charcoal gray ones, the pin-striped gray ones, and the black ones. As she moved the sixth navy blue one that looked remarkably like the other five hanging next to it she heard herself say aloud, "Lord only knows why I thought I needed another blue power suit."

Kate abruptly froze in her revelry.

From somewhere in a drawer of memories she hadn't opened in four years she heard Nikki's voice, strident and exasperated. "Why do you need another suit, Kate? You've already got enough to go a month or more without wearing the same one twice."

That memory was followed quickly by Nikki's voice asking the same question about all of Kate's other endless quests and acquisitions. Kate remembered her stock retort: "It's not like I can't afford it" (whatever the "it" in question at the time might have been).

Then one last one welled up and hit her like a medicine ball in the stomach. "Why chase another promotion, Kate? Haven't you figured out yet that it's not about the size of the bank account you die with? We've gone from Atlanta to Chicago, from Chicago to Detroit, from Detroit to New Haven, and still you want more. You won't find whatever it is you're looking for after the moving van pulls away from the curb, Kate. If you don't have it in here"—Nikki tapped her chest—"you don't stand a prayer of finding it out there."

It was like dominoes all lined up in her mind. Once the first one fell, the others had no option but to click, click, click until the last one was down.

It was four years in the coming, but at long last Kate knew why Nikki Irving had thrown in the towel. If she hadn't gone to see Nora back in September, if Nora hadn't taken her over to Frank's nursery to say hello to Casey, if Casey hadn't invited her up to do the surprise visit at Burr and Nora's, if she hadn't forgotten to give Casey her sweatshirt back, if they hadn't spent the day digging up the trees in the holding fields, if she hadn't gone for Thanksgiving, if Nora hadn't refused to let them put Burr in a home, if Nora hadn't died, if she and Casey hadn't fought. It was all so simple, despite its intricacy.

And now that Kate Bingham had it figured out, there was no question what she had to do next.

Chapter 29

Kate showered and selected her attire for the day. She decided on a dressy pair of gabardine slacks and a cotton blend print blouse. She took a corduroy blazer off the hanger to slip into when she headed out the door. For footwear, she picked a pair of knit socks adorned with kittens and balls of yarn and sensible, comfortable loafers. The uninitiated would think that it was a dress-down casual Friday in the fall instead of a filing season Monday chockful of appointments with high-paying clients.

Next she loaded the carry-on suitcase with two changes of clothes similar to those she was already wearing and her travel kit of toiletries. A sweatsuit, a pair of sneakers, undergarments, pajamas, and slippers completed the inventory.

The clock on the face of the microwave told her it was still too early to go to the office, so for the first time in longer than she dared admit, she sat at the table and ate breakfast. Not a can of low-calorie fake nutrition or a milkshake made with a powdered mix, but a real breakfast of toast with melted cheese and a banana sliced into a small bowl. She poured her coffee into a ceramic mug—not her usual screw-top metal travel cup—and sat in the living room to drink it, not gulp it, while she watched the string of headlights on the highway below grow to an ever-longer line of slaves making their way to the anthill.

She tidied up the kitchen, grabbed her briefcase, topcoat, and carry-on bag, then caught the elevator to the parking ramp.

"Good morning, Bernice. I knew you'd be the first one in." The wall clock behind Bernice's desk showed six-fifteen.

"Good morning, Ms. Bingham." Bernice barely glanced up as Kate approached but then raised her head for a better look as she noticed what Kate was wearing.

"I know it's old-fashioned, Bernice, but I wondered if you have time to take a letter by dictation for me this morning?"

"Now?"

"Unless you're in the middle of something, yes please."

"Of course." Bernice followed Kate into the inner office.

Kate hung her coat on the tree behind the door and then wheeled her leather chair out from behind the desk so that it was in line with the two guest chairs that faced the work surface.

"Here, Bernice. You take the comfortable chair for a change." Bernice hesitated, but she saw that Kate was smiling and had already seated herself in one of the guest chairs that she had adjusted so that it faced the armchair, so she did as Kate directed.

"Who is the letter to?"

"To all three of the partners. Let's do it as an in-house memo. Eyes only."

"And what would you like me to show as the subject line?"

"Director of Operations, New Haven Field Office." Bernice was cool. She never batted an eye as she made the curls and squiggles that constituted her somewhat rusty shorthand.

In less than five minutes, Bernice laid her pen down. "Would you like me to read that back to you, Ms. Bingham?"

"No, I know you've got it down perfectly. And if you think there's something that could be said better, feel free to work your magic on it. I'll sign a couple of blank letterheads that you can use to print it out on." Kate opened a drawer in the file cabinet to the side of the credenza and extracted the sheets. She used the mahogany pen from the set that flanked her nameplate to ink her name just below where it would appear in letter gothic typeface on the laser-printed pages. She extended the signed, blank leaves to her secretary. "Thanks, Bernice."

Bernice made a move to rise from the chair, but instead canted forward so that she was nearer to Kate.

"I realize this is none of my business, Ms. Bingham, but are you sure about this?"

"I've never been more sure of anything in my life, Bernice." The look on Kate's face left no room for doubt.

"Is there anything else, then?" This time Bernice did vacate the chair.

"Do you have time to book me a flight, get me a room, and reserve a car for me?"

"Certainly. What city and when?"

"New Haven, this morning. You know the hotels I like. Book me a room at whichever of them you feel like calling. I hope the ten o'clock flight is still on the schedule. Leave the return flight open." Once again, if Bernice found the request at all out of the ordinary, not so much as a flicker of astonishment registered.

"Obviously I'll need to clear your calendar and get someone to cover your appointments."

"Right. Thanks. I'm sorry for the extra work, Bernice."

Kate moved the leather chair back to its original spot and made a quick check of her desk for anything she wanted to take with her. Ten minutes later, Bernice was back in Kate's office and handed her a neatly typed page showing a room reservation confirmation number at a downtown New Haven hotel, her rental car information, and the airline booking for a ten-twenty departure to New Haven, Connecticut, via Philadelphia.

"Thank you, Bernice. Perfect, as always."

"My pleasure, Ms. Bingham." Bernice turned to leave the office and go back to her desk.

"Oh, one last thing, Bernice . . ."

"Yes?" She pivoted in place.

"From now on, it's 'Kate,' OK?"

Bernice pulled her face into a grin. "Of course, Ms. Bing—I mean, Kate." She took two steps, then looked back at Kate. "I hope things work out for you."

With that, she was gone, closing the door behind her.

Chapter 30

"DeWitt, Scroggins, and Howell. Kate Bingham's office. Bernice speaking. May I help you?"

"Bernice, good morning. This is Casey Marsden. I'm sure Kate is with clients, but could you take a message to give to her for me?"

"Oh, good morning, Ms. Marsden. I hope you and your family are holding up all right. Your mother was a very special woman. I'm going to miss her."

"Thank you, Bernice. Mother always spoke very highly of you, too. We're doing all right, I guess. As well as can be expected. Thanks for asking."

"I'm happy to take a message for Ms. Bingham, but I'm not sure when I'll be able to get it to her. She's not in the office."

"She's not? Did she call in sick?"

"Oh, no. She was in very early this morning and then made arrangements to catch a flight. Oh wait, rather than me taking a message, let me give you the number where she'll be staying. You probably won't be able to find her for a couple of hours, though, because her flight didn't leave here till almost ten-thirty."

Bernice read Casey the number for the hotel in New Haven where she'd made Kate's reservation.

"Thanks, Bernice."

"You're welcome. Please tell your brothers and sisters I send my love and my sympathy."

As Casey hung up the phone, she reached for the phone book she kept in the kitchen drawer. She flipped a few pages until she found the map of the United States with area codes superimposed on it.

She held out hope for one last second, but there it was: area code eight-six-zero, the southern portion of Connecticut. She felt the blood drain from her brain.

Her night had been as tumultuous as Kate's. She had fought and argued with herself until she was no longer sure what her position was on any issue other than she knew she didn't want to spend the rest of her life without Kate Bingham. Just after eleven o'clock Monday morning, she finally gave in to her heart and called Kate's office, planning to beg Kate's forgiveness and pledging herself to find a way to work things out.

"I think we've lost her, guys," she said to Roger and Kit, who were lying in the sunny spot in the great room. She knelt on the floor next to the dog and buried her face in his neck. "I wouldn't have thought she'd have gotten gone so fast. I guess she wanted it even more than she showed." Casey struggled to hold back her tears.

"What was that old song Mother always used to sing whenever one of us kids whined about something not working out like we wanted it to?"

She hummed a note or two. "Got along without you before I met you, gonna get along without you now . . ."

But as God was her witness, Casey hadn't the barest trace of an idea how to go about it.

Chapter 31

Meanwhile in New Haven, Kate was like a woman possessed. She had two important pieces of business to accomplish, and with any luck, she could knock them both off Monday afternoon and catch the first flight back to Atlanta the next morning.

She guided the rental car from the airport to the downtown area and pulled into a parking space at the First Union National Bank on Crown Street at three forty-five. The lobby would close at four, but it shouldn't take more than ten minutes to get what she'd come for.

She barely kept from breaking into a full run as she left the car and headed for the double glass doors.

"Hi. I'm Katharine Bingham," Kate stated matter-of-factly as she showed her driver's license to the woman at the desk in front of the locked door leading to the safe deposit boxes. "I'd like to access box number one-three-three, please."

"Certainly. Do you have your key?"

"Right here." Kate produced her copy of the dual-key system necessary for opening the box.

"Fine. Just fill in this register." The woman offered the sign-in book to Kate. "Will you need much time? We usually lock up at four o'clock."

"No, I just need to get some papers."

The woman spun the cylindrical lock on the barred door and cranked in the right numbers. She escorted Kate to the floor-to-ceiling bank of boxes and inserted her master key into the top slot of box number one-three-three and tipped the tumbler. She stepped aside so that Kate could do the same with her key. She pulled the box from its drawer and led Kate to a cubby hole of a room. She set the box on the small table.

"Just push that buzzer to let me know when you're finished." She pointed to a lighted, raised button beside the door frame. She left the room, pulling the door shut as she went.

Kate lifted the lid on the box. Just as she had remembered, inside were three bulky packets of papers, an envelope containing a single page, and a small velvet box. She took all of the items from the box and moved them into her briefcase. She knew that she would have no further need of the safe deposit box, but she also knew she didn't want to waste precious time doing the paperwork to close out her account. That could be done later by mail and fax.

She gave the button by the door a quick thump to call for the woman to release her from the safe deposit lockup.

"I trust you found everything as you expected, Ms. Bingham," she observed as she swung the door open.

"Yes, exactly. Thanks very much." A few quick steps and they were back at the barred door, another cipher of the correct numbers, and they were back in the lobby.

"Have a nice evening."

"You, too," Kate cast over her shoulder as she reached the exterior doors.

One down, one to go. From the bank, Kate negotiated a handful of turns until she was in a parking lot across the street from the Northeastern Property Management and Realty office on Grand Avenue. Rush hour traffic was beginning to build, so she prudently went to the corner and crossed with the light.

"Hello." Kate nodded to the receptionist. "Is Paula Neesom in?"

"Why, yes. She just got back a few minutes ago. Was she expecting you, uh"— the receptionist struggled for a name—"Ms . . . uh, I don't think I caught your name."

"Oh, sorry. It's Bingham. Kate Bingham. No, she wasn't expecting me"—Kate gave a half laugh—"but then again, neither was I."

The receptionist looked at Kate like she might be some kind of nutcase, but nonetheless excused herself to see if Paula Neesom would like to have her shown to her office.

"Right this way, Ms. Bingham." The receptionist gestured to the area behind several tall potted plants where a cluster of cramped offices constructed out of plywood gave the illusion of privacy.

"Well, Kate, this is a surprise. I hope there's nothing wrong at your rental condo down on Sergeant Drive."

"Not as far as I know, but that *is* why I'm here." Kate dropped into the chair that Paula was pointing to. "How would you like a new listing?" If either woman had hoped for small talk, there was none to be had.

"You're not going to sell that gold mine, are you Kate? That's one of the fastest-appreciating zip codes in the state. And even if it weren't, where would you ever get another view like that?"

"Even when I lived there, I was rarely home enough to enjoy the view. And if prices are on the upswing it sounds like the perfect reason to sell. Tell the couple leasing it that, if they want first crack at it, I'll give it to them for what it was appraised for at tax time last year."

"Oh, Kate, that's cheating yourself. Give me three months and I'll get you an offer at least twenty thousand higher than that."

"I'm not really all that interested in making a killing, Paula. I just want to get it off my list of payments to make every month."

"Well, you're the boss." Paula reached for a listing sheet. "Will you be buying something else in the area?" She couldn't keep the dollar signs from rolling hopefully past her eyes.

"No, I'm hoping to become a Southerner full time."

Paula began filling out the pertinent information on the legal-sized multipart form.

"Any chance you'd consider holding a specific power-of-attorney on this transaction when it goes to closing? If I can, I'd like to avoid another trip back up here just to sign a bunch of forms in a lawyer's office."

"I've done that a time or two, Kate, but it's not something that's common practice."

"I'll make it worth your while, Paula. It would save me a thousand dollars in airfare and at least that much in aggravation." Once again, the dollar signs spun in the real estate agent's eyes.

"You *have* been an awfully good client . . ."

"Then let's just make it a gentlewoman's agreement, OK? I'll write you a check, payable to you *personally*, not to the company"—Kate caught Paula's eye to be sure she understood the clarification—"before I leave today. I'll need you to have the paperwork drawn up. When it's ready, call me and I'll give you the address to send it to. We can use an overnight courier to get it back and forth." Kate estimated it would take an hour's time to get the power-of-attorney drawn and another hour at the settlement table. Certainly a thousand dollars an hour should be sufficient compensation for all of Paula's efforts.

"Will you be at your usual number in Atlanta?"

"I hope not. Take this number down instead." She gave Paula Casey's number in Delano.

"Eight-two-eight? Is that a new area code in Georgia?"

"No, that's just over the North Carolina line, about two hours north of Atlanta."

Paula jotted the number in her file, then went back to plugging data into the listing agreement. "OK. Now, what do you want me to put as the asking price?"

"I was thinking three-forty."

"I'm going to suggest you go with three hundred and fifty thousand. If you're willing to sell for three-forty, the buyers will feel like they're getting a deal when they counter-offer."

"Fine, Paula. Let's just get it on the market."

With the early sunset of winter, it was already dark by the time Kate had initialed and signed every necessary piece of paper to make it known that her two-bedroom ninth-floor waterfront condominium on Sergeant Drive in New Haven was for sale.

Now that both tasks on her two-item to-do list had been accomplished, she registered the fatigue—physical, mental, and emotional—that threatened to overwhelm her. She plodded to the rental car and covered the few miles to the hotel.

From her room, she called room service for a chef's salad and a piece of chocolate pie. She took a quick shower while she waited for the cart to be pushed to her door. The shower refreshed her and took the edge off her weariness. While she ate, she reviewed the documents she had reclaimed from the First Union National Bank earlier that afternoon.

First, the hardest one, which also happened to be the shortest one. She extracted the single page from the business envelope. Kate read the bold print at the top of the form aloud. "Certificate of Death. Raymond Eugene Bingham. Rock County, Wisconsin." Dry-eyed, she refolded the page and reinserted it in the envelope. "I miss you, Pop."

Next, she picked up the thickest of the other three bundles. It was her father's will. She scanned the pages until she came to the section that always made her heart stop. "I hereby devise and bequeath any real property of which I am possessed and all the rest, residue, and remainder of my estate, both real and personal of every nature and wherever situated of which I may die seized and possessed to my youngest daughter, Katharine Lorraine Bingham, if she should survive me. If she should fail to survive me, I direct the court to appoint an administrator to dispose of all such assets and further direct that the proceeds from all dispositions are to be bequeathed to the American Cancer Society."

Kate was no less shocked by the words on the page as she read them that evening than she had been the first time she heard them in the attorney's office in Janesville after her father died. She skipped ahead to another section in the will.

"To my other daughters, Martha Minerva Bingham Cates and Jolene Annette Bingham Wilshire, I bequeath the sum of one dollar each. For reasons satisfactory to me, I have chosen only to benefit the beneficiaries designated herein and to the extent so designated."

The date behind her father's signature was less than three months after Kate's mother had died. Until she and her sisters were in the attorney's office for the reading of the will a month after Ray Bingham passed away, none of them knew that he even had a will. They all expected one of two things: if he had a will, it would direct that his three daughters should share equally in the proceeds from the sale of his farm and his machinery and whatever else he might own. If he died intestate, the laws of succession in Wisconsin would have caused the same outcome. Kate relived the scene. Martha and Jolene were livid; Kate was too stunned to speak. Her sisters impugned Kate for cheating them out of their inheritance, implying that Kate had somehow coerced their father into making this "bogus will" as Jolene kept calling it.

Kate had tried to point out that the will was dated nineteen years earlier and kept repeating that she didn't even know he had a will. Furthermore, they had seen him hundreds of times more than she had through the years since their mother had died—how was it that she had accomplished this dastardly deed without them knowing anything about it? Her sisters were in no mood for reasonable explanations. Kate's already tenuous connection to them was all but severed in the attorney's office that afternoon in June six and a half years back.

Kate remembered a conversation she had had with Nikki shortly after returning to New Haven after that incident in the attorney's office. She had asked if Nikki thought she should just sell the farm and her father's other property and divide the proceeds up three ways to appease her sisters.

"Why would you do that, Kate? He had a reason for doing what he did. Who would you rather please, your dad or your money-grubbing sisters?"

So Kate had continued renting out the farm to the neighbor's son, Ron Bjornson. In the year and a half between putting her father in the home and his death, she sold whatever of his farming equipment remained to Ron at a fraction of its market value. She felt that was a better choice than having it rust and rot in the outbuildings.

One of the remaining two packets in Kate's briefcase was the deed to the farm. Her parents had purchased it right after they married. "Wow, last year would have been their golden wedding anniversary," Kate commented to herself. Once her mother was gone, there had been no need to keep track of things like that. Kate felt a sudden sadness creep in for all the celebrations that never happened.

The deed revealed that the Binghams had paid the staggering sum of three hundred dollars an acre for the land, which must have seemed a king's ransom at the time. Kate had received the current real property valuation statement with the annual tax bill in early December. By Kate's calculation (and she was an accredited accountant, so she was pretty sure it was correct), it now was worth six times that much.

In the years since her father's death, she had considered liquidating the holding and disposing of the profits in any of several ways—a trust fund for her sisters' children (it wasn't their fault their mothers had pickles crammed so tightly up their butts); an annual gift to the cancer researchers; a scholarship fund for young men and women planning to study agricultural sciences, to name a few. None of them ever seemed quite right, though, and so the deed sat in her safe deposit box awaiting some future fate.

Kate laid the deed aside and drew the last sheaf of papers from her briefcase. It was a life insurance policy. Name of the insured, one

Raymond Eugene Bingham; name of beneficiary, one Katharine Lorraine Bingham. The policy was underwritten by the company that had insured every vehicle her father had ever driven as well as his house against fire, his worldly goods against theft, and his crops against hail damage.

"The company will pay the principal amount shown in the Schedule of Policy Benefits and Premiums to the beneficiary upon receipt of due proof of death of the Insured and will grant other benefits, rights, and privileges as provided in this policy." The date next to her father's signature on the application page which was stapled to the policy showed that he had taken it out within days of when he had prepared his will. His wife's death had, quite obviously, spurred him to take action relative to his own demise.

When Kate was stripping the house bare after placing her father in the care facility, she had come across the policy among other legal documents that he kept in a metal box on the floor of the closet in his bedroom in the old farmhouse. Knowing the probable reaction from her sisters to her being the only beneficiary, she had never said word one about the policy—and that was *before* she knew the terms of her father's will.

When Ray Bingham died, Kate called an insurance agent in New Haven to ask "hypothetical" questions about redeeming a life insurance policy. Was there a time limit on cashing it in? What happened if a policy was found years after the insured had died? The agent told her that it varied somewhat from state to state, but that in general, there is a seven-year statute on life insurance claims. Most companies do an annual cross-match to see if they have any unclaimed, inactive accounts. If no one steps forward to redeem the policy within seven years, the money is forwarded to the state's general operating funds.

It might have been guilt, it might have been grief, it might have been inertia, it might have been uncertainty about what to do with the pay-out, but for whatever reason, Kate still had her father's life insurance policy (which she always thought was a somewhat amusing misnomer since "death insurance" was a much better description.)

She only had until June to do something about it if she didn't want it to become a windfall for the Badger State cretins currently occupying the statehouse in Madison. She finally had a good idea about what to do with the one hundred thousand dollars her father had left her when he shed his earthly form. She just hoped Casey would think it was a good idea, too.

All that was left of the lockbox treasure trove was the two-inch cubed velvet box. Opening it opened the floodgates to feelings Kate could barely name let alone master. Inside was a ring—a plain white gold band with a very simple setting holding a small blue topaz gemstone. It was the only thing of her mother's that she had. Her dad had asked her to help him pick out a present for him to give his wife on her fortieth birthday. They had gone all the way to a jewelry store in Madison to find it. Neither Kate nor her father knew or cared that blue topaz is the birthstone for December. As a January baby, her mother should have been honored with a garnet. If her mother cared that it was the "wrong" stone, she hid it well. She wore the ring as though it were the crown jewels.

When their mother died, Martha and Jolene swooped in to claim anything that might be useful or valuable. With great foresight, her dad had already taken the blue topaz from the jewelry box and, after Martha and Jolene had picked everything else fairly clean, he slipped the ring to Kate.

"She knew I didn't have taste enough to tell vinegar from salt," he said with typical self-deprecation. "But she always told folks that her prince of a husband had picked this out for her 'twenty-ninth' birthday. You should have it, Kate. I know you two didn't see eye to eye on much, but she was your mother and she loved you, more than you'll know."

The goddess of irony was working overtime, it seemed. Kate had to stop to think for a moment because the days had been such a jumble of late, but yes, today, January twenty-third, would have been her mother's seventy-second birthday. "Happy birthday, Mom," Kate whispered. "Thanks for the ring." Kate slipped the ring on her finger and was instantaneously struck by the sensation of someone kind and compassionate holding her hand. Too weary to contemplate all the mystical possibilities, Kate just let the tears work their healing ways.

She reassembled all of the papers and returned them to her briefcase. The tears abated as she clicked the latches and set the briefcase back on the floor.

The trip down memory lane had been draining, but Kate wanted to place one phone call before she gave in to her body's screaming request for sleep. She checked the time on the bedside clock. With the hour's time difference, she decided it wasn't too late to call. Directory assistance for area code six-zero-eight had the listing she needed. She used her calling card to dial the number. Soon she was hearing the broad, flat consonant sounds that the Midwest was famous for. The conversation went exactly as she had hoped it might. She ended the call by giving Ron Bjornson, the tenant on the Ray Bingham farm, Casey's phone number and assuring him she'd be looking forward to hearing from him soon.

Kate dearly wanted to hear Casey's voice. "She's probably still furious with me," Kate reasoned as she tumbled into bed. "It's better to wait to do this face-to-face, anyway." Kate wallowed down into the luxurious mattress. "I'm not sure I know how to sleep a hundred and thirty-seven dollars' worth," she grumbled with a yawn.

Kate took one last look at the clock and did a quick tabulation. "It's nine-thirty now. Flight leaves at seven. Four hours to Atlanta. Three—no better make it four hours from the airport to Delano—" Before Kate could count forward the hours on the clock, she gave way to the arms of Morpheus.

For once, Kate got her money's worth of sleep in a hotel bed.

Chapter 32

Kate settled into her seat on the plane. She let the events from the previous day circle through her mind while the jet queued up on the runway for takeoff. For the past six or seven months, she had told herself that, because the transfer back to Atlanta came up on such short notice, she hadn't had time to clean out the safe deposit box before she left New Haven. Besides, the papers were as safe under lock and key there as they would be in a comparable institution in Atlanta. And then of course, there was the more compelling reason that there were inklings that DS & H might offer her the office director's position there. Why bother closing out her accounts at First Union National of Connecticut—or for that matter, selling her condo—if she'd be back in a year or maybe two? And even if that promotion didn't come through, hadn't Paula Neesom told her that an ocean-view unit like that was a wonderful investment?

It was time to drop the delusion. While there was a grain of truth to those rationales, the real reason was that she had hoped Nikki

Irving would come to her senses and come home, and when she did, Kate would be ready. The more she thought about Nikki, the more remote and unworkable such a reconciliation seemed. Not only would it not have been feasible, Kate acknowledged, it was also unwanted. Nikki and New Haven were part of the past, like Janesville and the farm. And much as she had taken steps to close the door on New Haven for good, in another few weeks, she would do the same for Wisconsin.

To Kate's delight, the flights were smooth and on time. Once in the terminal in Atlanta, she dodged and ducked around people and wheelchairs and buggy carts and luggage as quickly as she could and caught the shuttle bus to the lot where she'd left her car. She gave fleeting thought to stopping at home to get some additional clothing, but decided against losing the time.

"Hell, for all I know, Casey won't even let me through the door when I get there," she worried to herself. She chased the thought from her head and prodded the Volvo to eat the miles a little faster.

It was nearly four o'clock when she exited off Highway 441 near Delano. She had no idea if Casey would be at her house or at Burr's, but hoping for the best, Kate decided to try Casey's house first.

She crested the hill at the top of Casey's driveway and caught sight of the moo mobile under the carport. Then she saw Casey and Roger playing fetch in the side yard and her heart skipped a beat, whether from fear or anticipation, she couldn't say—probably both.

The car hadn't stopped rocking on its suspension before she was out the door and vaulting the distance between her and the woman she loved.

"Casey, I've been such a moron. I'm so sorry. Will you forgive me?" The words flew out of Kate's lips.

"No, I'm the one who was wrong. Oh, Kate, when I thought you were gone forever—" Casey's words tumbled out on top of Kate's.

"I love you; the only thing I want is to be with you. Please tell me we can try again." Kate couldn't hold her tears at bay.

"I love you, too, babe. I tried to call you yesterday, but Bernice told me you'd gone to New Haven and I knew right then that I'd made the biggest mistake of my life. Oh, Kate, please don't go without me." They were wrapped so tightly around one another that they could barely breathe.

Kate loosened her grip enough to pull her head back so that she could see Casey's face. "If you want to go to New Haven, you'll have to go alone."

Casey took a half a step away from Kate so that she could look closely to see if she was joking.

"What?"

"I've told DS and H that I won't take the job in New Haven."

"Oh, Kate! Won't that make them mad? I mean, you told me you had to take that job to get the promotion you wanted—"

"It doesn't much matter if it makes them mad or not. I not only turned down the job in New Haven yesterday, I turned in my resignation."

"But that means you won't get the junior partnership." Casey was proud of herself for remembering the right words to describe the plum Kate had been hoping to pluck from the accounting world tree.

Kate put her palm gently under Casey's chin. "I'm not really interested in their stinking junior partnership. The only partnership I want is an equal one with you, if you'll have me, that is." She didn't dare draw breath until she heard Casey's answer.

"Do you mean it, Kate? The two of us . . . ?"

"Well, more like the six of us," Kate began but was interrupted by the creature at her feet. Roger had been circling their legs for the past several minutes and was not about to be ignored much longer.

"Six?" Casey asked as though it were a word from a foreign language that she was hearing for the first time.

"Here's three of us," Kate laughed as Roger relished the full body rub down she was giving him. "Two kitty kids in the house brings it to five." She stood so that she could look Casey in the eye to finish her statement.

"And your dad makes six."

Chapter 33

"I know it's only been two days, but it feels like an eternity since I've kissed you." Kate and Casey—with Roger doing his version of the Macarena around their feet—had made their way into the house. "I tried to tell myself we hadn't been together long enough for me to feel so awful about your leaving, but I was wrong." Casey clung to Kate, caressing and kissing her as she spoke.

Casey shucked her shoes onto the mat beside the door. Kate stepped out of her loafers and light as a feather laid her toes on top of Casey's feet while they stood wrapped in one another's arms.

"I know what you mean, Casey. I ached for you so much Sunday night. I wanted to call you, but I knew you'd just hang up on me. I almost did it anyway, though, just so I could hear your voice." Kate stroked Casey's face with the tips of her fingers. "I can't believe how close I came to ruining the rest of my life." She slipped her right hand behind Casey's head and drew Casey's lips near her own.

The kiss was all-consuming. Instantaneously, both women knew that there was only one reasonable next move. Wordlessly, they began their trip from the great room to the bedroom. It was a slow, ardor-filled journey. They would manage a step or two and then give way to the need to see or feel or kiss another place on each other's body. Piece by piece, they stripped one another of every article of clothing, leaving each garment wherever and however it happened to fall.

"You are the most beautiful woman on the face of the earth, Kayrun Marsden." Kate used Casey's given name so seldom that hearing it spoken aloud with such fervor only intensified Casey's arousal. Kate pressed Casey up against the hallway wall and kissed the hollow of her neck. She tenderly petted Casey's breasts while she used her mouth and tongue to explore Casey's upper arms and torso. In a slow, deliberate motion, Kate drew her left hand down Casey's abdomen and slipped it between Casey's legs.

Casey moaned in anticipation. "I have never wanted anything more in my life," Casey whispered, each word separate and distinct, as though it took great concentration to remember how consonants and vowels come together to form sounds. "Please, Kate."

Kate took her right hand and grasped Casey's splayed fingers. "Come on, babe." Feet must have touched the floor to convey them the final distance into the bedroom and onto the bed, but all either of them knew was that in an instant, they were on the mattress, and then, in the next blink of an eye, Casey was gasping for air.

She grabbed a fistful of Kate's hair with one hand and clamped the other hand on Kate's lower back. For that moment in time, there was only one entity, one being, one soul. The merge was complete and completely satisfying. Kate, her head wedged in the crook between Casey's neck and shoulder, tasted tears. She neither knew nor cared if they were hers or Casey's.

"Kate. My wonderful, marvelous, astounding Kate." Casey shifted beneath Kate's body. She felt as though she were reentering the earthly realm from some spiritual place, galaxies away.

"*You're* the real miracle, Casey," Kate countered.

As normal sensation began to return to Casey's arms and hands, she pulled the pads of her fingers in long, sweeping arcs up and down Kate's back, occasionally arching her hands so that her fingernails made brief contact with Kate's skin. Kate found the effect both mesmerizing and electrifying.

"I could lie here like this forever," Kate murmured as she turned her head to the side, freeing it from where it had been resting and resettling it just below Casey's chin.

"Huh-uh." Casey lifted her hands so that they were beneath Kate's shoulders. "I want you on your back, woman." Smoothly, she rolled Kate from atop her and eased her down onto the bed and in the same motion drew herself into a seated position next to Kate. Kate drank in the radiance of Casey gazing down on her. The look of adoration on Casey's face was beyond anything Kate had ever experienced.

"I love you, Casey, more than I ever dared dream I could love anyone."

Casey leaned over and kissed Kate tenderly. "Thank you for coming home."

"Thank you for letting me."

Casey lay back down and then momentarily stretched out full length beside Kate. In a twinkling, she moved to the end of the bed. She bent her head forward over Kate's feet and started slowly swinging her head so that the ends of her hair brushed almost imperceptibly over the surface of Kate's skin. Inch by inch, she worked her way up Kate's body until she was near enough to reach Kate's lips with her own. The kiss belied either of them ever having felt so much as a glimmer of passion before. It seared through them both like the fast fuse of a bomb.

Just when Kate was sure Casey would ease her yearning, Casey reverted to the end of the bed again. This time, she used the tip of her tongue to slowly, erotically trace the entire five feet seven inches of Kate's body from the farthest end of her toes to the top of her forehead. Kate was writhing with expectancy, but was too far lost in the power of Casey's tonic to utter a syllable and plead for release.

Once again, Casey dropped to the foot of the bed. On her final pass, Casey used her strong, broad hands to knead and embrace each muscle and joint, every crevice and rise on Kate's physical form. If ever a woman belonged totally to another woman, Kate Bingham belonged to Casey Marsden.

At long, loving last, Casey gave in to her need to fully, unreservedly satisfy Kate. As Kate arched her back in the crescendo of her climax, Casey felt her own body answer and echo. They lay drained and delirious in one another's arms.

Time passed—maybe a minute, maybe an eternity. There was nothing to say, nothing to fear, nothing to contemplate.

Bundled safe and snug together, they dozed off and awoke to find the sun nearly gone behind the horizon.

"I love you, Kate." Casey stretched and yawned.

"Lucky me." Kate grinned as she hugged Casey tight. "I love you, too."

And with that simple declaration, they got up and retraced their steps to the great room, retrieving their clothing as they went.

Chapter 34

"Where *is* your dad?" Kate asked as she slipped back into her shoes.

"Margie is staying all week. She's over at the house with him. I said I'd be back over to help with supper." Casey glanced at the clock on the bookshelf.

"Do you think she'd be OK alone with him for a couple of hours more? There's a lot I'd like to talk to you about."

Casey was so glad to have Kate back in Delano, she'd have granted any wish in her power. "Let me call over there and see how things are going."

Casey left Kate on the sofa while she called her sister from the kitchen.

"No problem." Casey smiled. "She said to just skip coming back tonight, so I'm yours, all yours." Casey rejoined Kate on the sofa. "I am, you know." She kissed her deeply.

"I don't think I recognize that ring, do I?" Casey pointed to the blue topaz on Kate's right hand.

"I barely recognize it myself. It was my mother's. I got it out of my safe deposit box while I was in New Haven." An idea blazed across Kate's mind. "This might seem kind of strange, I guess, but . . ." Kate pulled the ring from her finger. "Would you wear this as sort of a sign that we're together?" Kate blushed like a teenager on her first date.

"Hold that thought; I'll be right back." Casey jumped up from the sofa and vanished down the hallway to the bedroom. "I'll wear it on one condition," she said as she returned. She extended her hand, palm up toward Kate. "I'll wear that one if you'll wear this one." The ring in Casey's palm was one that Kate had seen on Nora's hand on several occasions. It was an emerald in a stylized setting on a gold band.

"We've been sorting through Mother's things. Christine and Margie and Judy will split up the rest of her jewelry. This is the only piece I took. I always loved the color." Casey held the ring so that the light played off the gemstone. "It was her birthstone. She'd have been sixty-two in May."

"Shouldn't we get matching rings to make this official?" Kate's need for symmetry reared itself momentarily.

"We can if you want, but I think this is a nice way to honor our beginnings." Casey grasped the ring in her palm and held it as an open circle. "Kate, be my home, be my lover, be my best and only girl from now until forever." Kate lifted her left hand so that Casey could slide the ring on her finger.

"Now you," Kate offered. "Thank you for knowing me better than I know myself and for loving me in spite of it." Kate placed the blue topaz on Casey's left ring finger.

"May I kiss the bride?" Casey didn't need to wait for Kate's answer.

"Too bad we couldn't dress the cats up as flower girls," Kate giggled as the newlyweds snuggled on the sofa.

"Nah, they'd have eaten the petals," Casey declared.

"Much as I'd like to have a repeat of our recent honeymoon"—Kate canted her head toward the bedroom they had vacated only a few minutes earlier and smiled broadly—"I really do want to ask you some questions about a whole bunch of stuff."

"I've waited my whole life for you, Katharine Lorraine. Now that I know you're really, truly mine, I can wait another hour or two to reconfirm what I tried to show you a little while ago." Casey kissed the back of Kate's hand. "What's on your mind?"

"Well, this will seem like the horse behind the cart now, but I wondered if you think I should keep my place down in Atlanta. I mean, you maybe aren't ready to have me here full-time, so maybe I should wait to sell it until you're sure about us."

"I'll let you know when I'm ready for you to move in." Pause. Pause. "OK, I'm ready. I've been ready since October, but for a bright woman, you can be so dense sometimes. I might consider letting you out of my sight for a little while now and again, but if I never have to watch you disappear down this driveway again, that would suit me just fine."

Casey cocked her head like a dog that can't quite make out the sound that it's hearing. "If you've resigned from Dewey, Screwum, and Howe, what are you going to do about work?"

"For right now, nothing. I figure there's so much to do over at your parents' house that I can make that my full-time occupation until it's done. You cannot imagine what it feels like not to have the vise of filing season tightened around my head for the first time in twenty-three years." Kate pressed the heels of her hands against both temples to demonstrate her point. "Of course, next year at this time, I'll probably be like a junkie in need of fix, craving the rush that comes from cranking out cases like crazy. I was thinking I might open my own little accounting office right here in Delano. I wouldn't want it to be a big deal, just something to keep my brain cells from rusting together."

"I know this will seem a little crass, Kate, but what are we going to live on? Love and good looks are fine as far as they go, but they don't pay the mortgage or buy the puppy chow. I won't start back at Frank's nursery until March, or maybe later if we have a tough winter."

"I don't think it will be an issue, sweetie." Kate set about outlining for Casey the various financial aspects of her (no, make that *their*) life. Even though she had resigned, she would get a severance package from DS & H; it was part of her contract. There was the sale of the property in New Haven. There would be the sale of the property in Atlanta. There was her dad's life insurance. And, as soon as she got word from Wisconsin, there would be the sale of the half section of land that her father had bequeathed to her.

"My God, Kate. That's a fortune." Casey paused and then chortled softly. "My mother always wanted her daughters to marry well. She must be laughing her ass off wherever she is right now."

"I've got some ideas about what I want to do with a chunk of the money when it comes in. If you don't like this, or if I'm being too pushy, you've got to promise you'll tell me to back off. I don't want us to start out our life together fighting about money."

"Try me."

"I want to remodel the house—this house, I mean. When I go back to work, I'm going to want a room that I can use for an office, or maybe even set up an office here to see clients. We both just hate the kitchen because it's so dark and cramped; I want to completely gut it and start fresh. If your family comes to see your dad, they'll need a place to stay and this house sure can't hold more than one or maybe two guests at a time. I want us to bring your dad here as often as we can so that he can stay with us and feel like he's still part of a family, so we'd need to have a room for him. And we could put unvented gas log fireplaces that burn propane in this room and in our bedroom and in the new guest room so that if the power goes out, we can just light them with a match and still be warm.

"I haven't touched a piano in years, but I want to get one and make time to play again, so if we added a little soundproofed music room I could practice without disturbing anyone. If we redo the laundry room, we could set it up so that there's like a little anteroom that Roger can hang out in when we're gone and we'll put a doggie door to the outside so that he could go outside whenever he wants to. And we'd want to put up a fence so that he wouldn't run away while we're gone for work or driving to and from the home with your dad or whatever." Once Kate started describing her dreams for the house, there was seemingly no end to the possibilities.

Kate pulled a pad of paper from her briefcase and showed Casey some of the floor plans she had sketched on the plane ride between New Haven and Atlanta. The two of them sat at the table and came up with a half dozen more. They made lists of all the features they wanted to be sure to tell the contractor to include. Casey caught the fire from Kate and soon was making notes of the various decorating touches she could envision employing in making their dream home a showplace as well as a love nest.

Even the animals knew that joy had returned to the house tucked in the woods outside Delano. Roger camped beside one or the other of his best human friends throughout the evening, and was only content if he was lying so that he was touching at least one of them. Caboodle and Kit slouched on the women's laps—or more frequently, on top of the sheets of paper from the drawing pad—and purred their approval.

"And we could knock these windows out here in the great room and make bays out of them with ledges for the cats to have sun baths." Kate was still on a roll.

"And we could talk till dawn, but I really do want to lie with you in my arms at least some of the night." Casey laid her hand across Kate's mouth lovingly. "You're sure this is what you want to do with your money, Kate?" Casey still couldn't quite believe the phenomenal turn of events that had come her way.

"I am. And it's our money, Casey. At least as far as I'm concerned."

"What you said about having my dad here . . ."

"According to the Internet, there are lots of new medicines on the market that really seem to help Alzheimer's patients. Maybe one of them will let him still have some good years. And even if the drugs don't help, I think we can work things in such a way that this house feels safe and familiar to him. He likes the animals, and they're good therapy. With both of us here to watch him, it won't be so tiring. Of course, it's your call, Casey. I'll go along with whatever you think is best. I'm right here with you every step of the way."

"But it doesn't seem very fair, Kate. You'll be pulling almost all of the financial load around here, and you've already had to go through all this broken brain stuff with your own dad. It doesn't seem right that you have to do it again."

"It all feels very right in here." Kate tapped her chest—much as Nikki had done when pointing out her frustrations with the "old" Kate. "I don't think I did such a good job with my own father. I'm lucky to have another shot at improving my record."

"I don't know how I'm ever going to repay you, Kate."

"I know of two things that will go a long way."

"What are they?"

"When the time comes for me to go back to Wisconsin to take care of the sale of the farm, I want you to pack an overnight bag and go with me."

"OK, I guess that's doable. What's the other thing on the list?"

"Take me back to that magical platform bed of yours and prove to me night after night that I've made the right choice for a life mate."

Casey wasted no time in making the first installment on a debt she hoped she never paid in full.

Chapter 35

It was the second week of April before all of the logistics for the sale of Ray Bingham's farm were worked out. By then, Burr had been at Morning Sun over two months and was doing reasonably well. Since he hadn't taken any of the dementia drugs previously on the market, he was eligible to participate in a clinical drug trial of a new product that had shown great promise in early testing. It was too soon to know if it would slow the progress of his Alzheimer's, but the Marsden children (and the newest "in-law") were optimistic.

Casey had gone back to work at the nursery in early March, thanks to a mild winter in the mountains. Her employer had agreed to grant her a two-day hiatus so that she could accompany Kate back to Janesville. The plan was to fly out on Sunday, April eighth, close on the property on Monday, fly back to Atlanta late that evening (spending the night at Kate's condo), and then drive the final leg between Atlanta and Delano Tuesday so that Casey could return to work on Wednesday morning.

They were already in the routine of checking Burr out of the Morning Sun facility on Sundays and spending the day with him, but since they would be away this Sunday, on Saturday, the seventh, the women picked Burr up from the home and brought him back to the house for several hours. Casey's sister Margie from Alpharetta (happy for a weekend away from her husband and son) had agreed to pet-sit while Kate and Casey were gone. It also gave her an opportunity to see her father. She was already at the house when they got back from Asheville with Burr.

Casey was like a schoolgirl preparing for a field trip. She packed and repacked her overnight case six times Saturday afternoon and checked and rechecked that her camera was loaded and that she had enough spare film about as often.

Following yet one more pass at her suitcase, along about mid-afternoon, Casey took Burr back to the small bedroom and encouraged him to lie down to rest for a while. She turned on NPR and sat with him till he dozed off. In another hour or so, they'd have to take him back to the home; the trip always seemed to go more smoothly if it was done as the first event after a nap.

"Sure you don't want to dump everything out of your suitcase and put it all back in one more time, Casey?" Kate ribbed as Casey emerged from the hallway.

"Yeah, what if you've got one brown shoe and one black one? Or one that ties and one that slips on?" Margie chimed from the easy chair where she was curled, thumbing through one of the interior design magazines Casey had bought to look for even more decorating ideas she might be able to use once the house renovation got underway.

Both Kate and Margie had teased her mercilessly all day about her struggles in deciding what to pack.

"Very funny, both of you, but no, I think I'm ready this time."

Casey plopped onto the sofa in the great room where Kate was already sitting with both cats in her lap. Roger, who had been looking out the front window, seized the opportunity to make the family grouping complete and spread out on the floor right in front of them.

"Well, here we are. The lesbians at home," Casey said lightly. "Hey, Margie! Grab my camera and get a picture of all of us. We keep saying we want a family photo, but there's never anyone here to snap the shutter."

Margie obliged. She picked up Casey's camera from the table and took three or four shots of Kate and Casey with their hairy three-some of animal children from different vantage points in the room.

"There, that should make the perfect picture for your Christmas cards next year," Margie predicted as she put the camera back in its bag.

The three women chatted about routines for the animals, how things were going at Morning Sun, who had heard what from other siblings, and passed a pleasant hour.

"I think I hear Daddy." Casey cocked her head toward the rear of the house.

Two and a half hours later, they were back from taking Burr back to the nursing home.

Dinner (courtesy of Many Fortunes carry-out), a few games of hearts, a little more conversation, and then it was bedtime.

"Have a wonderful trip, you two," Margie called from the door very early the next morning as Kate and Casey struck out for the Atlanta airport. "See you Tuesday afternoon."

From Atlanta to Chicago, Chicago to Madison, Madison to a rental car, and the rental car to Janesville.

"When my sisters and I were little," Kate explained as they headed out of Janesville, "whenever we rode with my dad, he'd call out the route we followed to get home. 'From town, it's six miles south, one mile east, half a mile north, second driveway.' I can still hear it in my head."

During the plane ride, Kate and Casey had decided that they should take a drive out to the farm so that Casey could have a look at where Kate had spent her childhood. Now that they were almost there, Kate was beginning to question the wisdom of that decision. Once she had moved her dad off the farm and into the home, she'd never been back, not even when she came to visit her dad or after his funeral.

"This is it," Kate said simply as she wheeled the rental car off the county road into the driveway.

How could a place look exactly the same as she remembered it and yet look nothing at all like the place she'd called "home" for the first eighteen years of her life?

An old, arthritic dog lying on the front porch of the house lifted his head and offered a half-hearted "woof" as the car's tires crunched over the gravel. It was enough to rouse the people in the house.

"Hello. What can we do for you?" a tall, rangy man pulling on a stained, billed cap bearing a John Deere insignia called as he ambled down the steps of the porch. (Of course, it sounded more like "Hullo. Whut can weee dew fore yah?" given how out of practice Kate was at deciphering the brogue of her mother tongue.)

"You're Ron Bjornson, right?" Kate held out her hand to him. "I'm Kate Bingham."

"Oh, my heck!" (No doubt as close to an expletive as the man ever got, Kate surmised.) "I hadn't figured to see you until tomorrow morning at the lawyer's office in town."

"A friend of mine made the trip with me." Kate gestured toward Casey, who was standing by the open passenger door of the rental car. "I thought I'd show her the old place, if that's all right."

"Well, for sure. It's still your place after all, well, at least until ten o'clock tomorrow." Ron grinned. "Most of the field roads are already in pretty good shape. We didn't get much snow this winter so the mud hasn't been too bad. Some of the hollows are still kind of wet, but you can get most anywheres you'd want to."

"Oh, I don't think we'd planned to do anything more than just take a quick look from the yard here—"

"Now that you're here, might as well take the nickel tour, don't you think?" Ron pulled his head sideways toward the rental car.

199

"That puddle jumper might not get you too far. Take the truck." He pulled his head the other way to indicate a mud-caked farm vehicle parked near the small building that used to house the well pump. "Keys are in it. You know your way around."

"If you're sure you don't mind . . ."

"Not a bit. Help yourself." Ron Bjornson looked down at his boots before continuing. "It was real decent of you to offer to let the rent I've paid since I started working the land go toward the down payment. I know that wasn't part of the deal we made when I took the place over. I don't think the bank would have come through with the financing if you hadn't done that."

It was Kate's turn to contemplate her footwear before speaking. Even with that concession, she would walk away from the settlement table with almost five hundred thousand dollars, so she was hard pressed to think of her gesture as particularly magnanimous. "My dad would have wanted the place to go to someone who appreciates it. Glad I could help out."

They both knew better than to say anything more or they'd be standing there blubbering like babies in the barnyard, and that would be very un-Wisconsin-like of them.

"Better get going if you want to see all three hundred and twenty acres before you lose your daylight." Once again, Ron used his head to point to the truck.

Kate and Casey climbed into what had once been a light blue Chevy pickup. As though she'd driven it only the day before, Kate double-clutched to get it to go from reverse to first and, with a wave to Ron as he mounted the steps back to the house, they set off to explore what for fifty years had been known (and would still be known for at least another thirty years to come) as the Ray Bingham place.

Casey glanced at Kate as she took them out of the yard and down the first of several rutted lanes on the farm. There was no mistaking that she was the farm girl come home.

"Dad always had a herd of feeder cattle back here. I used to drive the tractor to pull wagons with bales of hay out here to feed them." They bounced a ways farther. "For a while, this was the hog pasture, but Ron plowed it up to make another field. Looks like he planted corn last year." A few more turns and jostles. "This used to be wheat as far as you could see. Everybody plants soybeans now. Less trouble with blight and insects and a better pay-out at harvest."

They came to a grove of trees in what looked to Casey to be the middle of nowhere. "Come on, I want to show you something." Kate bumped the driver's door open and stepped out. The ground was a little soft underfoot, so she picked her way carefully. Casey followed in the imprints Kate made. As they got nearer the trees, Casey could see a small pond tucked down in a low spot in the center. "When it was hunting season, I'd come down here and pretend that I could put a big glass bubble over the top of this so that the ducks wouldn't fly out of here and get shot. It was always one of my favorite places."

And so it went down the twists and turns of the narrow lanes. Every little ways, Kate would offer her commentary and remembrances. Casey was grateful that she could busy herself taking lots of pictures as a diversion because she could do little more than say "uh-huh," or "I see." She knew if she attempted to say anything more, she'd start crying, and what would be the point of that?

It was nearly dusk when they chugged back into the farm yard and Kate stopped the truck in the spot they'd taken it from a lifetime earlier. She hit the horn button lightly once. Ron came to the door of the house and opened it enough to poke an arm out to wave good-bye. "See you in town tomorrow," he reminded her unnecessarily.

The women got in the rental car to head back to Janesville where they'd taken a room at a motel just a few blocks from the attorney's office where the closing would take place.

"Just to make it official," Kate intoned with a half-laugh, "back to town is half a mile south, one mile west, six miles north." She paused. "You taught me well, Pop."

"Kate, I don't think you should sell your farm." Casey finally trusted her voice enough to speak more than two syllables. "I can tell you still love the place."

It took Kate a moment to let her thoughts gel and to be sure her own voice would hold up. "I love my *memories* of the place, Casey. Now that I'm grown and gone, I can look back on it as my perfect childhood home. I'll always have it in my heart, but it's time to let it go. I'm glad you convinced me to come see her one last time"—she reached over to find Casey's hand—"and I'm really glad I got to see her with you, but I'm ready to be done with it and let it be what it really is—the past." She cleared her throat. "My real home is with you back in Delano."

They made the turn onto the main road back to Janesville.

"And six miles north," Kate repeated, knowing it was the last time.

Chapter 36

"How long do you think the closing will take?"

"I'd say an hour and a half. Will you miss me?" Kate kissed Casey warmly as they lay in their bed at the motel on the morning of Monday, April ninth.

"Of course." Casey kissed Kate in return.

Two hours later, as soon as Kate left to walk to the attorney's office, Casey took the keys to the rental car. She had two stops to make and only an hour's time in which to do so.

First, she went to the mega-drugstore she'd seen on the edge of town as she and Kate made the drive to and from the farm the day before.

"Do you have Wisconsin souvenirs?" she asked the clerk behind the check-out counter at the front door.

"You bet. There's a coupla shelves of 'em on aisle eleven."

Casey hastened to the location indicated by the clerk and eagerly scanned the merchandise. "Just what I wanted!" she cheered as she selected a small wooden box with a removable lid. It was cut in the shape of the state of Wisconsin. A little red heart was painted on the box in the approximate location of Janesville. The words "keep Janesville in your" were imprinted above the heart.

Casey paid for the box and steered the rental car out of town. "Six miles south, one mile east, a half mile north" Casey repeated to herself over and over as she drove. She recognized the driveway into Kate's farm. She checked her wrist watch. Yes, it should still be Kate's for maybe another twenty minutes.

She turned down the first of the roads to the fields the way she and Kate had done the previous afternoon. Just a short distance down the lane, she stopped the car and got out.

Casey knelt at the edge of the field. Using a spoon she had "borrowed" from the continental breakfast bar at the motel, she scooped the rich, black soil into the wooden box she'd purchased not fifteen minutes earlier. The box couldn't hold more than three tablespoons, total, but it was enough. Casey tucked the box back into the plastic bag from the drug store and tied the handles of the bag into a tight knot.

She was already picturing in her mind's eye the three-dimensional collage she'd make for Kate's birthday in August using the pictures she's taken as they roamed the farm in Ron Bjornson's pick-up yesterday and this keepsake container of dirt from the place that Kate called home in her early days.

Casey found her way back to the motel and had all of seven minutes to spare before Kate came into the room.

"How did it go, sweetheart?"

"Couldn't have been better. If Ron Bjornson were a man given to gymnastics, I honestly think he'd have done back flips when the attorney said, in what I suppose passes for a lawyer's version of humor, 'Congratulations, Mr. Bjornson; you just bought the farm.' "

"No regrets?"

"Only that I didn't fall in love with you sooner, Ms. Marsden."

Kate hugged Casey hard and promised herself she wouldn't cry. "Now, let's get on the road. We've got a plane to catch."

As they neared the Madison airport, Casey posed a question that had been burning within her. "Don't you want to at least call your sisters while you're here, Kate?"

"No. They'd want to know why I was here, and when I told them, they'd just get all pussfaced and ugly. In a funny sort of way, I'm feeling really relieved to be free of the responsibility of owning the farm. I don't want to ruin that by letting Martha and Jolene try to rain on my parade." Kate guided the rental car into a spot at the agency's check-in location. "Maybe I'll look them up the next time we come to Wisconsin."

In their heart of hearts, both Kate and Casey knew that, almost certainly, the next time they were in Wisconsin would be the weekend after the twelfth of never.

Chapter 37

"Oh, phooey! I can't believe he managed to ruin this picture."

The trip home from Wisconsin had gone like clockwork. As planned, they had stayed in Atlanta overnight Monday and then gotten an early start for the drive back to their house on the hilltop in the mountains of western North Carolina. On their way through Delano, they had dropped Casey's four rolls of film at the one-hour processing lab at the Delano drugstore. By the time they got to the house, assured the animals that they were back to stay, said good-bye and thank you to Margie, and unpacked, it was time to dash back into town to grab a bite to eat (for once, not from Many Fortunes) and pick up the developed pictures.

Kate emerged from the kitchen where she was putting pizza and salad on plates and joined Casey at the dining table in the great room. "What's wrong with it? It looks fine to me." Kate made a cursory review of the snapshot that Casey was holding. It was the one of the two of them sitting on the sofa with the animals gathered around them that Margie had taken the day before they left for Wisconsin.

"Look again," Casey directed. "See? Right here—" She pointed to the background of the photo. "We thought Daddy was asleep, but he wasn't. He must have been going from the bedroom to the bathroom. That's him in the doorway."

Kate leaned over Casey's shoulder to get a better view. "I'll be darned. He's in every one of them, isn't he?" She thumbed through the other similar shots on the table in front of Casey.

Because he was moving, Burr's image was blurry and out of focus. The opening to the hallway was surrounded by a framed doorway that obscured about half of his profile.

"And these were so good of you and me and the kids," Casey moaned.

Kate looked at the photos one more time. "You know what, love? I don't think we could have gotten a better representation of what our life is like right now if we'd staged it."

"Come again, Kate?"

"Here we are, you and I, front and center, happy as can be in our home with our wooly wannabe children. And there, still part of the scene, but not fully present, is our other family member—half a man, out of focus and barely on the fringe of whatever is happening around him."

Casey reflected on Kate's deduction. "How about that? You're absolutely right." Casey sat back in her chair; Kate bent forward and laid her face alongside Casey's for a long moment.

Casey held the picture out at arm's length and studied it again. "So this isn't a lousy picture after all," she concluded.

"Not at all," Kate assured her. "In fact, I'd say it's picture perfect."

About the Author

Jane likes to joke that she and P. D. James have something in common—both were long-time civil servants who reached the conclusion that writing novels is far more satisfying than working for the government. Jane spent much of her tenure with the federal government in Washington, D.C. In recent years, she has lived in Georgia. She is now approaching the end of her career with one of the country's largest federal agencies. Following retirement, she plans to devote her time to writing books and tending her gardens.

Jane is the youngest of six children. She was born and raised in a farming community in northwestern Minnesota. She received her elementary education in a one-room country schoolhouse; she holds a Bachelor of Arts degree from St. Cloud (Minnesota) State University. She is a member of Lambda Iota Tau, an international literature honors society. (The *lambda* part is purely coincidental.)

Jane and her life partner—and far more cats than reasonable people would ever acknowledge owning—reside in the foothills of the north Georgia mountains. When she's not at the keyboard working on her next novel, you'll find Jane either at the piano (where she is teaching herself to play, albeit about four decades too late) or out in the woods, feeding the deer and the birds and watching for signs of the red fox whose den is on their property.

Picture Perfect is Jane's first novel.

Publications from
BELLA BOOKS, INC.
The best in contemporary lesbian fiction

P.O. Box 10543, Tallahassee, FL 32302
Phone: 800-729-4992
www.bellabooks.com

ABBY'S PASSION by Jackie Calhoun. 240 pp. Abby's bipolar sister helps turn her world upside down, so she must decide what's most important.   ISBN 1-59493-014-7 $12.95

PICTURE PERFECT by Jane Volbrecht. 240 pp. Kate is reintroduced to Casey, the daughter of an old friend. Can they withstand Kate's career?   ISBN 1-59493-015-5 $12.95

PAPERBACK ROMANCE by Karin Kallmaker. 240 pp. Carolyn falls for tall, dark and . . . female . . . in this classic lesbian romance.   ISBN 1-59493-033-3 $12.95

DAWN OF CHANGE by Gerri Hill. 240 pp. Susan ran away to find peace in remote Kings Canyon—then she met Shawn . . .   ISBN 1-59493-011-2 $12.95

DOWN THE RABBIT HOLE by Lynne Jamneck. 240 pp. Is a killer holding a grudge against FBI Agent Samantha Skellar?   ISBN 1-59493-012-0 $12.95

SEASONS OF THE HEART by Jackie Calhoun. 240 pp. Overwhelmed, Sara saw only one way out—leaving . . .   ISBN 1-59493-030-9 $12.95

TURNING THE TABLES by Jessica Thomas. 240 pp. The 2nd Alex Peres Mystery. *From ghosties and ghoulies and long leggity beasties* . . .   ISBN 1-59493-009-0 $12.95

FOR EVERY SEASON by Frankie Jones. 240 pp. Andi, who is investigating a 65-year-old murder, meets Janice, a charming district attorney . . .   ISBN 1-59493-010-4 $12.95

LOVE ON THE LINE by Laura DeHart Young. 240 pp. Kay leaves a younger woman behind to go on a mission to Alaska . . . will she regret it?   ISBN 1-59493-008-2 $12.95

UNDER THE SOUTHERN CROSS by Claire McNab. 200 pp. Lee, an American travel agent, goes down under and meets Australian Alex, and the sparks fly under the Southern Cross.   ISBN 1-59493-029-5 $12.95

SUGAR by Karin Kallmaker. 240 pp. Three women want sugar from Sugar, who can't make up her mind.   ISBN 1-59493-001-5 $12.95

THE FALL GUY by Claire McNab. 200 pp. 16th Detective Inspector Carol Ashton Mystery.   ISBN 1-59493-000-7 $12.95

ONE SUMMER NIGHT by Gerri Hill. 232 pp. Johanna swore to never fall in love again—but then she met the charming Kelly . . .   ISBN 1-59493-007-4 $12.95

TALK OF THE TOWN TOO by Saxon Bennett. 181 pp. Second in the series about wild and fun loving friends.   ISBN 1-931513-77-5 $12.95

LOVE SPEAKS HER NAME by Laura DeHart Young. 170 pp. Love and friendship, desire and intrigue, spark this exciting sequel to *Forever and the Night*.
ISBN 1-59493-002-3 $12.95

TO HAVE AND TO HOLD by Peggy J. Herring. 184 pp. By finally letting down her defenses, will Dorian be opening herself to a devastating betrayal?
ISBN 1-59493-005-8 $12.95

WILD THINGS by Karin Kallmaker. 228 pp. Dutiful daughter Faith has met the perfect man. There's just one problem: she's in love with his sister.   ISBN 1-931513-64-3 $12.95

SHARED WINDS by Kenna White. 216 pp. Can Emma rebuild more than just Lanny's marina?
ISBN 1-59493-006-6 $12.95

THE UNKNOWN MILE by Jaime Clevenger. 253 pp. Kelly's world is getting more and more complicated every moment.
ISBN 1-931513-57-0 $12.95

TREASURED PAST by Linda Hill. 189 pp. A shared passion for antiques leads to love.
ISBN 1-59493-003-1 $12.95

SIERRA CITY by Gerri Hill. 284 pp. Chris and Jesse cannot deny their growing attraction . . .
ISBN 1-931513-98-8 $12.95

ALL THE WRONG PLACES by Karin Kallmaker. 174 pp. Sex and the single girl—Brandy is looking for love and usually she finds it. Karin Kallmaker's first *After Dark* erotic novel.
ISBN 1-931513-76-7 $12.95

WHEN THE CORPSE LIES A Motor City Thriller by Therese Szymanski. 328 pp. Butch bad-girl Brett Higgins is used to waking up next to beautiful women she hardly knows. Problem is, this one's dead.
ISBN 1-931513-74-0 $12.95

GUARDED HEARTS by Hannah Rickard. 240 pp. Someone's reminding Alyssa about her secret past, and then she becomes the suspect in a series of burglaries.
ISBN 1-931513-99-6 $12.95

ONCE MORE WITH FEELING by Peggy J. Herring. 184 pp. Lighthearted, loving, romantic adventure.
ISBN 1-931513-60-0 $12.95

TANGLED AND DARK A Brenda Strange Mystery by Patty G. Henderson. 240 pp. When investigating a local death, Brenda finds two possible killers—one diagnosed with Multiple Personality Disorder.
ISBN 1-931513-75-9 $12.95

WHITE LACE AND PROMISES by Peggy J. Herring. 240 pp. Maxine and Betina realize sex may not be the most important thing in their lives.   ISBN 1-931513-73-2 $12.95

UNFORGETTABLE by Karin Kallmaker. 288 pp. Can Rett find love with the cheerleader who broke her heart so many years ago?
ISBN 1-931513-63-5 $12.95

HIGHER GROUND by Saxon Bennett. 280 pp. A delightfully complex reflection of the successful, high society lives of a small group of women.   ISBN 1-931513-69-4 $12.95

LAST CALL A Detective Franco Mystery by Baxter Clare. 240 pp. Frank overlooks all else to try to solve a cold case of two murdered children . . .   ISBN 1-931513-70-8 $12.95

ONCE UPON A DYKE: NEW EXPLOITS OF FAIRY-TALE LESBIANS by Karin Kallmaker, Julia Watts, Barbara Johnson & Therese Szymanski. 320 pp. You've never read fairy tales like these before! From Bella After Dark.   ISBN 1-931513-71-6 $14.95

FINEST KIND OF LOVE by Diana Tremain Braund. 224 pp. Can Molly and Carolyn stop clashing long enough to see beyond their differences?   ISBN 1-931513-68-6 $12.95